THE TRADERS

THE TRADERS

Scott Shibuya Brown

Black
Lawrence
Press

Black
Lawrence
Press

www.blacklawrence.com

Executive Editor: Diane Goettel
Book Design: Amy Freels
Cover Design: Pilar Garcia-Brown

Published 2017 by Black Lawrence Press.
Printed in the United States.

For my mother

I.

How you do, my name is Cecil Po, I am 58 years in August.

For the long time, 19 years, my bookstall is at 182 Porridger Road, South District, Tandomon City, The Kingly Republic of Tandomon. Now it's big enough yes, but when it started it was just an alley space between a bad-smell coffee stand and the hairdressers' always full up with the Indo maids from the Atwells Lanes. But as time went by the coffee shop got shut down when another mouse tail got found again in the coconut *nian gao* (unluckily by the council official), and after Tandomon changed over to being poor, the maids went away and the hairdressers put up blocks, too. And so then I advanced into their spaces for during this time the other booksellers also got plowed by the bad econ and I purveyed much inventory very quickly and cheaply. And so if the front to my shop looks appearance-same from then, inside I now have three spaces run together on top by a catwalk upon which I learned to commove very fastly and without devoting too much thought. Ha!, and this name is funny to me for I do not regard cats so much for they bring me always bad luck.

But maybe you say I have bad luck, anyway. This might be true, too. Never I thought I go on being here twenty years. That would be like the jail sentence if you told me up top. I would have been very low or maybe even strike you if you would say this, for back then I desired only the single thing and that was to lock up myself in the prison of being a notable writer. So to this task I devoted many many hours and many many years and overall I completed for myself several long books of careful pages. But like the child's story of the girl with the *Xiasi* dog that just turn up its nose to food, all my tries got rejected from the book people. I joke to myself that sometimes my tries were rejected so fast the stamp paste on the envelopes was not yet dry. Now all the paste is dried-up and all my writings sleep underneath my bedframe and I forget about them.

But maybe you say I am in jail, anyway. Then again maybe you are right. Day after day I spend moving these piles of old books to here and there, shuffling hurting feet and trying to look busy when the customers arrive so they don't think they have come into a cannot make it shop. And then they go away without buying not even the paperback and I have wasted my efforts for nothing. Other times they come in and ask me bushels of questions wanting this volume or that one for a cheap price, and when I don't have or it is too much they change to huffy and walk out with no words. Meantime my stacks grow taller because when the persons come in with their don't-want volumes and cannot get you to buy they leave such behind anyway since no one likes to toss books. So now I am trapped wherever I move by the stacks of Mr. Robbins and Mr. Sheldon and Miss Collins because I cannot throw these away either, and now they become even more like my jailers since I slave myself to find space for them and their fat bricks of rubbishy writings.

So this is my trade and my bookstall is named Gecko 88.

All the same I have survived for these many years running my business and luckily have not yet perished. So much is thanks to my father, who though he is long ago passed, possessed a prime head in figuring and sums. He always instructed that a businessman should not stoop himself to selling products but instead trade his ideas. So I tongue-lash myself to always remember his words. And here I am lucky that my simple bookstall is not far off from the Ansleigh Secondary for Boys, which is here since before Tandomon was its own sovereign and still much the ace school. So twice a year before the college entering trials I fly a high banner adverting BOOKS FOR CRAMS! with a picture of cap and gown and a happy boy holding his paper, and I make sure every morning to litter the windscreens in the car parks by the school. And sure enough the next day the parents flood in like ants on the double to carry off my special-ordered sets on accountancy, maths, English literature, what have you. From this I harvest enough to float from term to term and have done so for twenty years next July.

Now I have a funny coincidence to tell you. Not all my books are rubbishy paperbacks or for schooltests. I have many solid classic volumes, too. Sometimes people collect books their whole lives but one day get tired of seeing them and want to sell all. I know this feeling of tiredness. Sometimes people die and their family don't care to keep their big dusty editions lying around and maybe think too, they must be valuable since the dead person went to the bother of collecting them. Now sometimes that can be true also so when this happens, no matter how I feel, even if too busy or too weary, I always make time to go look.

So one day I hear the low voice on the telephone asking me if I take away collections and when I say yes, I am informed this address in the Settlers Ward. It's the long-away trip and I don't make it for the few days but when I finally go I see much mourning going on because the dead man was a very old *Ah Pek* with many children and grandchildren and old aunties still wailing away. One fat man with a chicken backside then takes me to a dark room where there is a beautiful knockout steamer chest and inside it is full up with this dead man's books. There are not so many considering how long this man lived but all the books are solid–many Londons and some Kiplings and Maughams all covered up in shiny black leather–and so after my looking I make up my mind to buy. Maybe I don't sell them so quick but I think of the type of book that is growing taller in Gecko 88 and consider that these kind are better to change the character in my store. On the way out, the *Ah Pooi* says to me that such books look like new since they only lie on the shelf because the *Ah Pek* cannot read English. But this is not so unusual; I know this before, too.

My big surprise is when I go lug these volumes home. Because I have been in the book trade twenty years next July, I am knowledgeable from front to back about all the types of volumes printed and can expertly tell you about every kind of writer and everything this writer publish. Even those who write only one book and quit, I know their names. It is like the trick with me if you want to try my memory. Go ahead and test anytime. But in this *Ah Pek's* pile I see two books with a strange name mixed up with all the Londons and Kiplings and Maughams and what have you. It is a fancy one too, like the barrister or council official. This notable writer is named Mr. Lawrence L. McLemore.

Now I never heard this guy. And so because this is strange for me I pick up the volume to look closer. But then it hits me like bricks that I spied this name this very morning when lazing over my *kopi-o* before my shop opens. You see, even though I no longer want to be the notable writer, I still habit myself to buy such digests to keep atop this world. (Ha!, so maybe I don't forget everything about myself.) I send off by mail and when they arrive

I arrange the tall stack by the register and when no customers arrive I read everything word-by-word going very slowly.

First off there is the *South-East Asiatic Literary Review*, which is very boss and very official with big pages half the size of my bed-table. It takes me sometimes a few weeks to scan everything here and I don't ken one hundred percent either but luckily it arrives in the box only every two months. Then there is *Serious Books Digest*, which is not so long and not so *cheem*, but also not so interesting, either, and I go through this one very quickly. Overall the best for me is the *Indo-Asia Book Journal* because it is not so upper and the writers there can be very mocking and put on a humorous face when they think the book is unworthy. Sometimes I feel sorry for the notable writer they scold about but then I think to myself, Man, you write and publish your book! You got no complaint anytime! You're lucky some important reviewer take the time to read your writings. And I drink more *kopi-o* and go on to the next scolding.

So I was finishing up this magazine in my thoughtful mind when I reached the back page where they place all the adverts. Now I like this part of the *Indo-Asia Book Journal* like a boy likes his litchi candy and sometimes I read it two or three times over. Always there is the funny mash-up of people selling or wanting things, holiday houses to let, high-drawer institutions pitching themselves to students, and some lonely hearts adverting, too. Particularly I am interested in what people try to peddle off as valuable and also what kind of persons promote themselves for company. Once the while I even think that I should reply myself to this person or the other but then I consider all the trouble that maybe lies ahead and I close the page.

But since it is an important book journal the editors always keep one row of spaces in this mix bag for the people to make requests about the notable writers. As like, *I'm writing a historical account of Gabriel Fielding and would appreciate receiving information or anecdotes concerning his medical practice in prison* dot dot dot and what have you. Or, *I am seeking essays and short monographs for an edition on the feminine consciousness of Dorothy Richardson* dot dot dot and what have you. This space is always crammed up by the professors and lecturers from all the South East Asia schools, although what kind of information or anecdotes the local people can likely have about such writers makes me wonder. And never once do I hear the local persons busy at discussing the feminine consciousness of this author or that. Still these professors and lecturers keep asking, and now and again I even see pleas by the British teacher or the USA one.

And this is where I spy this writer's name. In this box halfway down the row is printed, *Currently seeking information about expatriate British writer Lawrence McLemore for a biography in progress. All personal correspondences and anecdotes welcome, particularly those regarding McLemore's experiences in SE Asia. All contributions will be acknowledged.* Then there's a postal box address for the USA in Michigan and after that this teacher's name and where he scholars: Prof. M. Mittman, Saylorsville Junior College.

Ha, so there is where I heard of the guy! I hurry off to find the journal in the shop to confirm and when I do, I look at the book more closely. It is named *My Stolen Life* and is an old one, circulated in 1937, almost forty years ago. The HK publisher is called Rumple & Co. and though it went down in the Pacific War, on this occasion or that I still cognize some books from this concern. Maybe they even some have writers around that people are still admiring about. I then scan number two book by this writer, which is even older, printed in 1933, but looks just as shiny since no one else looks at it, either. I leaf the book awhile, then glimpse the first page to check the title, which is *Footprint in the Water*, then close it and ponder awhile.

What kind of hell title is this, I think, for it strikes me strange that a notable writer that has important professors from the USA hunting after him should name his significant book like this. Next I start to laugh for such a thing reminds me of a children story or a naughty joke book I keep when young. Once the while I even sell a comic book like this to a boy who comes looking. And so now I feel ready to open up these pages and read some of the lines by Mr. Lawrence L. McLemore concerning what's on his mind since despite my quiet face, I like any good chance to break myself up.

But this becomes my mistake. Because when I get a few pages deep into the book I see it is one big mash-up. On one hand, there involves some big shot man who forgets his memory and gets twisted up with a *samseng* that knows the forgetting man from before and now goes to rob him but then gets hurt by a blade and dies. On the other, the forgetting man has a cheating *Ah Nia* girl-friend who also wants the money and runs off from him but then escapes a crack-up in a carriage and so switches her mind about the forgetting man, but then he's gone off to England or Horlan or wherever, and so she fling herself on a bed and cries for him and dot dot dot and what have you. I tell you this because despite its looks, this thing is a chore and after thirty, forty pages of this talking cock I tire myself out. The story turns and twists like bullshit and what one big event has to do with the other I am without clues and neither does Mr. Lawrence McLemore say either, and overall I waste a half-hour, maybe longer on this nonsense before I throw it aside.

And now my feeling changed. Not everyone like every book I know, but now I think this is a very rubbishy book and I start to feel the dislike of Mr. Lawrence L. McLemore. Beside him Mr. Sheldon and Mr. Robbins and Miss Collins write like Mr. Shakespeare, or even Mr. Hemingway. At least they don't give me the mash-up stories with sentences that scatter all over the place like drunk butterflies and give me the hard time so I quickly suffer my pounding headache. How the world does this man publish this kind of thing, I ask myself, and why do important professors from the USA want to know about his life? My judgment says these books are the bust, no more worth it than a scratched-out drawing. I bet if you ask this man to write his own signature, he would *tua teow*. Yet for no reason he has two shiny books in black leather right next to Mr. London and Mr. Maugham, and the *Ah Pek* and all the children and grandchildren in the *Ah Pek's* house think he is just as notable and admiring because his name is sitting there on a high shelf to look at.

Now I start to feel myself provoked. I think of the books that lie peacefully under my bedframe that don't make it to the high shelf anywhere. All the years I write and write and send off to the John Sanderson Literary Agency, Inc. in HK but never get any soap there. They just rebound my requests faster and faster until they get tired and in the end don't bother to reply me anymore. Sometimes I think they have a smart secretary that does nothing but tear up the letters from people like me. And also the boss executive that arrows her to forget my calls. Once I even think I should circulate my writings myself (and I ticked all the notable writers who did this–Mr. Proust, Mr. Whitman, Mr. Crane) but maybe I got the lesser steel because after considering and considering, I rejected this idea. And so my books go back to sleep.

And now I recollect something else, too. Just lately the *South-East Asiatic Literary Review* printed the long windy theme that cataloged all the local estimable authors. This piece names off every country and so goes through a long list–Thailand, Malaysia, Indonesia, Burma, what have you. But when they come to Tandomon, the important editors leave it blank and say that no literature arises from that small country and so has none. Even Singapore not yet ten years old has a list of names and books. What is this, I think. How do they know everyone in Tandomon who pens compositions? The important editors must be all super-powerful to know this. True, I never heard of any Tandomon notable writers myself either, but maybe like spiny lizards they all are laying under rocks like me. Maybe they also write to the John Sanderson Literary Agency, Inc. in HK and get their manuscripts torn up. Maybe likewise they got piles of writings underneath their bedframes *kooning* away. We are all not lucky enough to get approved by the significant book people, you know.

As I chew over this, my feeling changes again and something else strikes my thoughts. For maybe the trying writer in me is not all gone case and could be I still have some power to invent my words. Not used in awhile but maybe still there. Just the other day in fact, I scribbled the urgent reply to the important editor of *Serious Books Digest* who was complaining like devils that he failed to receive any of my subscription cheques. But because this is not the first grumble he sends me, I was much stirred and so my pen fired back the strong return. Unfortunately I needed to throw such away after reviewing my accounts, but all the same it was a powerful barking response he was lucky not to receive. Truth is, it became a surprise to me, too.

So why does all this thinking come to me now? Because as I sit in Gecko 88 holding this copy of this cannot read notable book and the beg from the USA scholar wanting more hungry information about the man who pens it, the new idea strikes me. For I think that if the Professor M. Mittman wants to hear so much about Mr. Lawrence L. McLemore, I would be glad to tell him the urgent things to make his book truly intriguing. Tandomon, after all, is the far-off place from the Saylorsville college and there is much a scholar like him needs to know about the life in these Asian parts, details that I can inform him, no sweat for me. And then if I do this I can get myself contributed as the notable Tandomon writer that once had the acquaintance with the famous *Ang Moh* author, so the next time the *South-East Asiatic Literary Review* wants to print the same story again they cannot say we all are lizards under rocks here. The next time the list for sure has got the one name, and now I think that maybe this even strikes the blow for all the Tandomon writers. This seems to me as everybody winning.

And the more I consider my urgent idea the more I decide it is affirmative.

So taking up my number one prime stationery and my best black biro, I begin to inscribe my careful note, like a boy chewing around the nut with the poison inside. It takes me just the few minutes and goes:

Dear Professor Mittman,
How do you do? My name is Cecil Po and I am glad to know your acquaintance. Allow me the chance to reply to your placed advert in the Indo-Asia Book Journal for information concerning Mr. Lawrence McLemore for your significant book. I am now in Tandomon City, Tandomon but growing up as a young man I knew Mr. McLemore, who was deeply acquainted with my father and a friend of his for many years. Due to this, I have many distinct recollections of him and his life that I will be glad to provide you if you are so interested...

II.

The day after I post off my careful letter to Prof. M. Mittman in Michigan USA I wake up at the crack and go early to sweat at my bookstall. I don't yet open Gecko 88 but instead drink the *kopi-o* I make for myself and puzzle over the sales book that for some reason is not so lively in the last month or so. I study and study and confirm and double-confirm but all the time it does not change and the figures just equate the same. I then try to call up some smart words from my father but cannot recall any and so my mood now begins to be worrying and I sweep away the record book in the low temper.

After awhile, though, I hear the knock on my door and my friend Charlie O. suddenly is there to talk about his life. But I am all right to see him since it diverts my mind and so I allow him inside and brew up a Lapsang pot since Charlie O. is from England, though that is years ago from when I first knew him and I don't think he even recalls this. It is the long time, all right.

Still not so much of him has changed over time. To tell about Charlie O. I would say that he is the good-heighted man that is also squash-shaped like the grown jackfruit and he wears a cheery face and a tall nose that wrinkles up when he laughs. He likes to take the big drinks in the afternoon and he also likes the mishap story where others is the butt. But despite that I would say I think he is the sad uncle inside. Usually is the same subject with him for he cannot find the person that loves him or wants to be with him and about this topic he goes on a long time. Giving him more problems is that Charlie O. is a homosexual man and must always take care to whom he talks. Once the while I see him beat up from speaking to this or that wrong person and it is a regretful thing to look at his torn-up face after. When I first know him years ago he asks me if this thing about him bothers me, but when he says this I do not know what to think, or more truly I do not think. Official people can say one thing but many *Baba-Nyonya* persons such as me do not care over who fucks the others. It is their doings.

Now he wants to tell me about his new friend that he has the problems with since this friend wants to go away to Thailand and leave Charlie O. here. It is a sad mess-up state all right and as Charlie O. talks about this his face truly looks low. It's my fault, I made a botch, he says in a whisper voice, and even though he has a red face and not so much white hair over his balding spot, sometimes Charlie O. reminds me of a little boy. This is a time like that and after he finishes he doesn't talk anymore and just drinks his tea, maybe dreaming if he could go to Thailand, too.

Actually though, I know who Charlie O. really wants to cry about. It is his old friend he had years ago when Charlie O. was still in his English college and that also left him, but even so he still talks about like he is right here. Even today I think Charlie O. waits for the return of this man that is named Mr. Goade and who I tease Charlie O. by saying Mr. Goat. As in once in a while expressing, "Any letters or telephone messages arrive from Mr. Goat?" Or, "Plane ticket come today from Mr. Goat, *meh*?" But this is only when Charlie O. is in a good mood, not like now.

Truth is though, I got no base to tease Charlie O., and more and more I think I should promise myself to quit. See, I too am alone for years and for the long while it was a hard thing, maybe as hard as the time now is with Charlie O. Like him I also missed the right *Ah Nia* when I was young and now it is too late and I no longer bother to look. Maybe it was because I was always the silent one with the nose in the book or maybe it was because I told myself I have lots more time for the marriage and was not so stirred-up about choosing. But because I was not careful and then got eaten up by the idea of being the notable writer, much time went by and all the women drifted off from me. Maybe too, my main thoughts about myself don't sound like true reality to them. However it occurred, my chances to talk with such flirting women got lesser and lesser until one day when I looked around and everyone was disappeared.

Of course this doesn't mean I was the hundred percent shut-in person either, for I always tried to recoup myself, even if such was like the old saying that the more one chases, the less there is for you to find. There is one time in particular that I remember like yesterday. It came because I had the young friend who likes to get together to chew the ideas about making the movies from the well-known Asian books. Now this is a far-out notion since back then Tandomon only recently acquired the picture business, but over this he was much stirred and we would chat for long times about the various plots from this or that spy book or adventure novel. He always says to me that if I could just write him the urgent script, we would be in the business.

At the same time he says these things, he always is encouraging me to go mingle myself and find an *Ah Nia*, even though I'm about ten years out-of-date by then. Plenty to fish he repeats, and in his case he always has a fresh *ger* to go with, and so I nod along even if inside maybe I'm not so sure.

Then one day he says that the big social scene is coming that I should not miss. Is the Leap Year day and the tradition says that on such a night all the *Ah Nias* will throw the big bash and go propose to the men. He says his friends already *chope* the table at a big hall and that I should follow. At first I am hesitating but the more he talks, the more he eggs me over what kind of mighty splash this occasion will be and how it is the once every four years opportunity, and so in the end I am convinced.

And now my thoughts begin to change. Maybe this is the right event for me, I think, since there will be plenty to fish and if the *Ah Nia* wants to approach me, she likely will listen to the thoughts I have and also not pay so much attention that I'm not so young like she. There live all types in the world, my father used to say, and no one knows who likes to be attracted to the others.

So considering this I make my plans, such as shopping a new white suit with extra double pleats since by now my dress-up clothes are all *obiang*. It's not so shiny like the fashion then but me and the salesman are both agreeing the shape is smart. I then make a special trip to buy the Fox's butter toffees wrapped up in the gold paper to hand to the *ger* who approaches me as a favorable gesture to seal my deal, though once I get this expensive box it begins to worry me. What would happen if more than one *Ah Nia* wants to talk to me? Do I show this right away or hold the box for later? I brood this over but finally think to hide it in the paper sack until I'm ready to give to the most deserving *ger*.

So finally the night is here and my friend is right since this is a much fancy bash at the *tok kong* hall in Lime Quay. I arrive and say *An Zhua* to my friend and he gives my name all around and they all reply, Glad I'm there and we exchange the greetings. So now I'm sitting at a big table and there is drinks everywhere and the dishes of *cze char* in front and again my friend is correct for soon some *sui Ah Nias* come floating up to our seats to chin wag everyone and take them away to more private areas or hustle them onto the ballroom floor where the band is playing and people now are gyrating away. It is exactly like my friend predicts and in my mind I recall the famous book by Mr. Scott Fitzgerald where there is the big party at the mansion and all the rich people go swimming among themselves enjoying their drinks and their chats. So it is A-okay and once the while I picture myself like I'm in this book, too, with my drink and new white suit. But that is until the time starts to fly by and all the sudden I see that everyone around me is disappeared and it's just me left at the big table with no one coming up, anymore. And when I glance around to the other seats I notice no one is by themselves, only me. Now and again someone glimpses over but then they look off like they don't want to cognize me and haste on.

Now as I sit there in my white suit holding my special gift to hand to the special *ger* I am there to meet, the hours start to drag longer. No one from my table is coming back and still no one arrives to talk to me, not even the serving boy to clear off where I'm at. By myself I try to grab some attention from this or that *Ah Nia* that sails by but they don't give no chance, either. Meantime I feel myself growing shamefaced and so now I also got to play like I'm drinking or doing something busy, but really I'm just feeling small and foolish, like my image is provoking people to laughing and thinking, "What you think you doing here, man?" It's a bleak feeling I got, like I'm the argly insect no one wants to glimpse or maybe just look at the one time to make the jokes about. Truth is, it gets very dismal and now the music is louder and everyone is gyrating away and busy enjoying themselves and long ago I finished my drink so my glass is empty. And so finally when the musicians stop to announce the lucky draw from the stage and everyone's head is turned to that way, I bolt off and make it to the door.

I tell you, I never felt so much relief as when that night air hits my face and I'm out of that social scene and commence to walking home. It's a far-off distance, maybe ten kilometers, but I'm not thinking what I'm doing and I start marching through the dark in my new suit, even going through the bad tenement areas. Sometimes a cyclo driver pulls along and asks do I want a ride but I wave him off, and sometimes someone shouts at me but I ignore that person too, and I'm almost home when I recall about that gold box of highway robbery candy I left behind on the table.

Once I get inside, I take off my new white suit with the extra double pleats and hang it away. A couple of days after, I sprinkle it with moth flakes and put it in the trunkcase with my old things and photographs I don't need anymore. I not look at it since.

But after this it's like my tries at meeting-up the women changes for me, like that was the dividing time. I still go on looking but now I just get the same reactions from all the *Ah Nias* as if they had the big meeting about me beforehand and agreed among them, and so after awhile I fade myself off. It's much easier on my feeling, I think, and around this time anyway I'm throwing myself like a devil into my bookstall. And so like the friend that dies and gets buried away, I don't consider this part of myself anymore.

So now all such matters are quiet with me and I just listen to the stories about the others' lives. But I think that everybody does this no matter if they get married or not, so maybe here everybody ends up the same. Like this one that just happened to the college boy whose father got the druggist stall across the way. We three are chatting one day and this boy says he's damn angry at his new *ger* who's a foreigner and doesn't speak much of the language. See, they going to meet downtown one night but she's mixed-up where she's supposed to be and goes to the wrong neighborhood place and then starts to worry because it's getting to be the long time and he's the no-show. And next she tries to call him but also don't get him. So then she gets all *kan cheong* and tries to grab the help from the policemen who catch no ball from her talking but get the idea that maybe he's done something bad and so they run off and arrest this boy and take him to the stationhouse. So she's waiting there when they drag him in but he's mad like a monkey cut off his tail and dresses her down right front of all the officers until she cries and cries.

Damn blur, he says of this *ger* and even now he's still much stirred-up, but as he's telling this, my mind doesn't pay attention to that story. Instead I'm wondering about this boy's *ger*, and what it must be like to have a *sui Ah Nia* like she running across the whole big city all nervous and flustered, just waiting to see you to make her cry out to be happy. Or standing somewhere dressed up on a jam-pack street anxious about you coming, and all lit up when you finally arrive and maybe then you also got an extra-special appointment for the rest of the evening. That must be something. That's the reward for life, I think, easy to overcome any problem. But this boy don't know the first thing about such because he's still the small one yet and not so aware; and only then do I cognize that neither do I know this thing, for not once had I that.

So now all this floats through my mind as I sit across from Charlie O. with his tea cup getting cold and hear his story again about his friend leaving and with his face about to break down once more. For some reason I'm glad he's pouring himself out to me like this. We're just two alone getting-older men, I think as I raise up to make up another tea pot. Why anyone else wants to listen to what we say, I don't know.

III.

A week or so goes by and again there are no customers in my bookstall one afternoon as I am absorbing from the *South-East Asiatic Literary Review* the mashed-up story of the artist that announces she devised a new way to read books, no matter the old way seems fine to me. This artist says she sets up four or five televisions in her front room and all of them show the sentences from the book, like the ticker-tape that scrolls by. So just by sitting in her room, after awhile she finishes all the words bit-by-bit. The order she reads them is not the point, she says; what's important is that she understands the mind of the writer by sinking down in the way he writes his words. She says in the future this is the way all the books can get read.

Ha!, I think to myself. If that's the case, my bookstall can come down to just a handful of TV boxes and I can rid myself of all these rubbishy works that burden my mind and take up all my precious space. No one would be interested anymore in opening up the volumes and leafing the pages to discover how a book was printed or when it got circulated or what the writer looked like. Such matters pass into history. These things can only attract the attention of the professors and lecturers who make their livings out of the past, not the regular people.

However, thinking about the professors also recalls to me the letter I have got from Prof. M. Mittman in the U.S.A. In his reply, the professor says he's glad to know my acquaintance and to get any of the good remembrances I have of Mr. Lawrence L. McLemore. He says his book project already is begun and off to the big start, and not to worry if I give him any papers or original material because he'll treat them carefully and return them quick. He also says how greatly he admires Mr. McLemore's writings and he ticks off the catalog of Mr. McLemore's books he's going to discuss. This last part gives me a surprise and also rises the feeling of jealousy in me. Mr. McLemore may not have so much writing power but I see he printed a lot of editions; this I have to hand him. Maybe such is the reason Prof. M. Mittman believes he is the notable writer.

The letter then closes with the professor hoping to hear from me soon and is typed on the paper from the Saylorsville Junior College in Saylorsville, Michigan USA so I can see everything is on the official level and he's not just playing play. The professor also signs it with the signature that looks like the mashed down spider and that tells me he's used to writing the significant messages like this.

So now I take this note out to scan again and maybe for the first time it strikes me that if I am going to reply Prof. M. Mittman from the USA, I will need the good stories full of the intriguing actions and urgent plots to feed his knowledge. At the least, I need to know the important history of Mr. McLemore's life so I don't confuse up my tellings and make Prof. M. Mittman drop my contributions. So tearing out the sheet from my accountancy book, I copy all the titles the professor wants to know about. Some of them still strike me that Mr. McLemore is having the big cock-up—*Potatoes in the Attic, The Barber Has Lumbago*—but Prof. M. Mittman ranks them

like they're important and since I only have two years at the pre-
fectural college I cannot argue with the university scholar. Then
even though it's still the bright part of the day, I lock up Gecko 88
and go to the Tandomon National Library est. 1914 through special bestowal of the Queen Mary, and where I have not been since
beginning my bookstall, twenty years next July.

In my mind it's not changed the one bit though all the books
now just look like regular volumes to me–not so mighty like
when I was young. It's still dark indoors like before and there is
the same smell of beat-up leather and falling apart pages, just like
my stall after the rain is over. Old books always got a stubborn
scent to them, it seems to me, like they're trying to argue back
they're still important.

Because it's burning up like the dickens outside, when I come
in I expect to find the big crowd of readers cooling themselves but
instead all I see are a few *Ah Peks* and some *Ah Mms* scanning the
gazettes with the couple of fans overhead whirring the air. Some
of them got their grocery bags like they're finished up shopping
and one's got the tied-up dog sleeping on the floor. Could be
like the scene from the old folks home, I think. After this I go
up the stairs but all along the big floor it's even emptier with no
one cramming the old books or no groups of unhappy students
drudging away at their schoolworks. I also try to look around to
find any coming-up notable writers from under rocks today but
I don't glimpse them, either. Overall it makes me think that the
future of Tandomon is in serious trouble if such derelict scenes
like this keep themselves up.

Now first thing I do is go hunting for Mr. McLemore's titles,
and since the professor rates them so highly, I expect the heavy
pile of dusty volumes to be waiting for me on the literature shelfs.
But after straying through the old-smelling aisles and finding the

place where Mr. McLemore's writings are supposed to be, I see that the whole Tandomon National Library est. 1914 possesses only the one name from my list–*The Crying Bandicoot*. This sets me back. Man, I own two times as many copies as the country's whole collection! My bookstall is twice as powerful as this institute and I started it myself, no thank you Missus Queen Mary. No wonder Tandomon is poorly off in its intellectual development if the officials can't be troubled to stock the significant writings, I think. I then take this book away, seat myself at a lonely table and break it open, and part of me is feeling bad for Mr. McLemore for being the victim of such low-minded national persons.

But truth is, this book's writing is even worse off than I recall, and after the few pages I'm catching ball why the Tandomon National Library est. 1914 is grudging any more accumulation of Mr. McLemore's writings. This one got the plot about a jockey who wins the race, but then falls off the horse cracking his head and so gets nursed up by an *Ah Nia* who's married to an old doctor who's got a grown-up son from a before marriage that's in jail for whatnot and needs to make a pile of money to desert to America, but then she gets to fall in love with him, and the jockey finds out about it and suddenly is mean and tries to make him pay the money instead and dot dot dot and my familiar suffering headache comes back to me and I throw the book down with like disgust. I then check the printing date and see that this one circulated in 1946 so calculating from the last, Mr. McLemore has been working his trade for ten years since and still it reads like the same rubbish. In fact, it's so ungrammatic that for several minutes I battle myself over whether to keep up with the idea I have with Prof. M. Mittman or if I should just flee from this botheration, especially since Mr. McLemore's writing seems to be getting worse the longer he accomplishes it.

But then I calm my thinking and consider that maybe I am troubling myself too greatly over the small matter. Could be I don't need to struggle through Mr. McLemore's worthless writings so long as I can get the grip over his life facts such as where he's born, where he grew up, where he did his schooling, and all the other what-nots and what have-yous. This is the type of grist that I think should mainly fill up Prof. M. Mittman's intriguing book. And such in any case is easier than plowing through all these drunk butterfly sentences that keep sprouting endlessly before me and are pounding my mind. So again I raise up, but this time to find the research on the notable persons.

This however takes me into the even lonelier place with the books that haven't been pulled for years and where no one looks like they have come visiting since, either. Such a scene strikes me like the empty museum I saw as a boy and afterwards had the bad dreams about the soldiers waving their long swords and knives and holding up their enemies' dripping heads. So now in this same vacant-like place, I dig and prod and get dusted up until I finally find the top shelf of giant pink volumes that weigh so heavy I almost knock myself out getting such down. Why the officials make these books so high and unreachable beats me, and in searching around I also see the Tandomon National Library est. 1914 is seriously deficient in its providing of beneficial step-rungs. But no matter, I climb up and handle them down carefully one-by-one and I am just about done when suddenly the raging man comes running up from nowhere to scold me to be careful with the bindings I am holding. He says I should be quiet since people are studying and reading their important books and this isn't the playground for me to be fooling around.

Now I look at this fellow hasting over and for the moment I don't think he's lecturing at me since so far I'm being careful with the old editions that nobody has come for the long time, anyway. But then I look through his eyes and see that I must look like the *suah koo Ah Chek* mixed up in the part of the library he doesn't belong. See, I come direct from my bookstall where I don't care how the others glimpse me so I am in my rubbishy pants and worn away shoes, plus my hair is all blown apart from walking outside. And tell the truth, I believe I also forewent my morning ablutions.

Still, he got no right to assault me like such so I bark back to this scolding man that I'm not playing but researching, and to make himself useful and go hunt down the supplementations to the editions I got, and for future's sake not file them away on the top shelf like they are vanished so the people have to go begging the officials. This is his job, I scathe him back, and now I am raising my voice and getting louder. See, being in the book trade twenty years next July has informed me to all manners of publications just like these dusty *Who's Who* for 1933, 1948, 1961, and 1970 that I am holding and that nearly knocked me down retrieving, and that people try to sell me sometimes claiming their old uncles or auntie is listed inside for something famous (though everyone knows such is world bunkum since if their old uncle or auntie was truly printed there, the person would be telling everyone they see, from all the neighbors to the strangers on the buses and never give up such a book and also try to get others to buy. Tandomon people are like that).

But from my special book experience, I likewise know that there is no such thing as the supplementations I have just mentioned about and since the scolding man doesn't want to reply to my face he doesn't know such, he's going to fluster himself for many minutes scouring for these. And I'm right about this because as soon as I scorch him the man turns pink like the fat

books I'm holding and goes off in the huff and I am in peace.
Tandomon persons are like that, too.

So now I stroll back to my empty table and open my giant
binding number one. For a comical moment it strikes me that
even if I take the workday off, I am still toiling myself in books.
Then again, maybe it's not so playful. But never mind, I forget it
and look up the oldest one. Ha!, I think opening it. This volume
was printed forty years ago and it took us this long to finally meet
up. But unfortunately there is no luck for me here, just the pages
of nobody, and so I put it away and crack the next from 1948.
And here I discover something to help my case. It's on top of page
number 271 and is not much of the listing but goes:

McLEMORE, LAWRENCE LLEWELLYN
*Born: Glasgow May 19, 1895; s of Norman Orrick McLemore and
Edith Cornelia (née Ebsworth).*
writer and explorer
*Education: Penang Free School, Malaya; University of Hong
Kong (BA 1917)*
*Career: Served in Royal Navy 1918-23; British Overseas Min-
ing, cartographer and explorer 1924-30, Ceylon, Malaya and Siam;
lecturer and second master Albion Secondary, Malacca 1930-1934*
*Publications: Footprint in the Water, 1933; My Stolen Life, 1937;
The Barber Has Lumbago, 1939; The Smell of Your Memory, 1946*
Recreations: Bowls, raising hedgehogs, swimming
Address: Regents Hotel, Anson Road, Singapore

Now this is exactly the kind of hungry details I need to devour
to get started and I copy them carefully beside my list of Mr.
McLemore's writings. Reading such I think it's a good thing for
me that Mr. McLemore has moved around a lot in these Asian

places since maybe Prof. M. Mittman isn't so knowing about such areas and I don't have to be one hundred percent *zhun* in creating my tales. Too much knowledge kills the cat, like they say, and if I want to be contributed in his notable book I always got to keep a lively story on the burner. I can already feel my thoughts stirring now with the things I could be creating.

I then crack open the next ten more years. Still the information is the same except the titles grow bigger. Now there is added:

The Crying Bandicoot, 1949; A Sandwich for Monty, 1952; Potatoes in the Attic, 1958

So even as I'm getting the growling stomach from reading these titles, I precisely mark these dates and then open the last big book. But here there is the surprise because suddenly I see that Mr. McLemore is no longer recorded alongside the others with the same name. And so I go slowly and double-check but his listing is still vanished and I turn the big binding around to confirm that I pulled the correct date. And just as I'm doing such, it flashes to me that Mr. McLemore is not here because he must have deceased since the last circulation.

How I know this I can't say, but all the sudden it strikes me like the for-certain fact and gives me the shock. Now, never at all did I think Mr. McLemore was still alive and writing books, but neither did I think he was dead somewhere, either. Truth is, I don't know what I was thinking. Except now that I realize this, a sad feeling starts to raise in me even if in my consideration Mr. McLemore is not so much the notable writer. Maybe ten minutes ago I wouldn't be so pitying but since then I know more about his venturesome life and could be now I'm the only one carrying around these vital details. That's a funny feeling, too.

So next I go back to the vacant aisles and begin hauling down more volumes to see the last time Mr. McLemore was listed in such. It takes until 1966 that I dig up his name again. Two more books are added up here–*A Sandwich for Monty: The Story Continues, 1962; Nestor Is My Podiatrist, 1965*–and also the address is changed. Now his mail is at the Wan Sai Hotel, Nong Khai, Thailand, a place I never heard before. But from this new information I also know to hunt up the other giant volume that is named *Who Was Who* and pull the binding for 1961-1970. And just like my sense of things confirms there is Mr. McLemore's name printed on page number 629 with the listing that states *Died September 1967*. There is no more information after this, not even the place where he got deceased or how it came about. But if the important publishers of such weighty tomes say Mr. McLemore is dead, then I think that such seals the case and so my urgent research on Mr. McLemore's past life I suppose is completed. And so with my feeling of being sad coming up even more, I stuff away my notes and close the book to leave.

IV.

Exiting the Tandomon National Library est. 1914, my mind is whirring like the ball of bees. Truth is, while the one hand regrets Mr. McLemore has been deceased, the other says my task now is chickenfeet since there is no living person to argue back when I write my good stories. So suddenly it looks like I got the free big hand to create all the kinds of events for Prof. M. Mittman to devour, and in fact some of these accounts already are arising in my mind as I tramp my long blocks back to Gecko 88.

But just as I'm about to turn the key to my bookstall and start penning my plots, I look across the way to the papers store and see Angry Lim shouting into his phone. He's angry even for him, which is how he got named since for the businessman who is supposed to treat the customer, Angry Lim is instead all the time mad and barking up trees. Never once is he irated with me though, only the looksee-looksee browsers who just mangle his goods without buying any, so I go over to have the look.

Walking in I see he's got the stack of printed sheets in his hand and he's raising such over his head like he's going to fling them around like the *siao* person all over his stall. Now about Angry Lim there's the handful of things it needs to be said; most primarily that despite his expressing a fiery face most of the time, the voice that comes out of it is squeaky like an *Ah Lian* schoolgirl so one must guard when hearing him not break out with laughing. And because he's always got the mouthful of ready outcries, this sometimes becomes the difficult chore. Also, Angry Lim never efforts himself so much at work but mainly likes to snore in his stall with his one eye kept open. He says this happens because one day he woke up and captured the foreigner trying to run off with the expensive gold fountain pen. Later though he changed the story and says he sleeps with his eye open because he has a pretty wife and wants to watch that no one can steal her. But you know I seen Angry Lim's wife, too. If I was he, I think I'd keep both eyes closed.

Now I am waiting until Angry Lim's fire goes out, though I am also studying the ceiling for awhile since his voice is squeaking like the rusty play swing worse than ever. I sometimes wonder if the cats and dogs go and crowd at his backdoor when he's mad like that. Finally though, it dies off and he tells me his trouble, which is that the big concern that ordered up the giant amount of his A-1 stationery went bankrupt and says they don't need his paper anymore, but also say they don't want his bill, either. They closed down and they're washing their hands so don't bother to send the charge, please. Angry Lim then tosses the bundle aside and wipes his crying-out face and moans why is he so *mong xing xing* that he takes the order from the *ai pee, ai chee* big-talker business people who in the end just all fart and no shit. He's a bad businessman, he says, not worth it to run his fancy store. If he didn't have a very beautiful wife, he goes on, he would throw himself in the sea this minute and again I have to go watch the ceiling.

But it's in the middle of staring my eyes upward that the sudden idea strikes me about Angry Lim's high-cost stationery. For I see that these papers and envelopes he now is waving around again are the purest white just like a coconut insides, and by the top is printed in flashy silver letters: *NEW PATHWAYS DEVEL-OPMENT & TRADING COMPANY~TANDOMON CITY, TAN-DOMON.* The look is top-flight like it's from an ace firm, not one just *pokkai.* And so before my brain can grab hold my tongue, I am asking Angry Lim how much he wants to sell me for the one batch. Maybe I don't want the whole thing but I'll take a little, I say. Right away Angry Lim's face perks and he forgets about throwing himself in the ocean and what his wife looks like, although I see some of him also is considering why I want someone else's fancy paper. He doesn't push too hard about this though, and after we deal backwards and forwards I leave his shop with my new sheets that I am fortunate to have secured so cheaply.

So why do I need this shiny labeled paper that I stack away in my important desk drawer soon as I enter my stall? Because now I am thinking that Prof. M. Mittman maybe won't believe my stories if he finds I'm only the barely make it bookstall man. How the earth can such a person know any notable writers? he would say, and he won't *pang chance* to me. But on another hand if I'm the considerable figure like the boss then I know for sure he would give me his full attention and pay close watch to my plots.

See truth is, I know from the book digests how hungry the scholars are for the stories from the official people. They like to say they don't want such accounts but the minute the significant person starts spinning the tales, the scholars eat up everything like the hawker stall ready to close. And then they kowtow themselves further to hear more. I think that maybe because the scholars aren't always so rich and notable, they like to feel important, like they're back and forthing with the powderful ones. And so if Prof. M. Mittman believes he is now conferring with the Executive President of the New Pathways business who is writing to him on these high-cost sheets, like before it's nobody hurting and everybody winning.

So late that night after Gecko 88 is shut up, I stay at my book-stall, open the light and use this paper to pen my story. It is my first one and it has been the long time since I tried to create my words so I give myself time to relax my mind to invent the most vital scenes. However, even though I am the patient man and am drinking cups and cups of *kopi-o* to stir my thoughts, each sentence soon becomes the labored struggle. I jot something, cross it, jot something else, scratch it and get stopped again. All the plots that were raining before now are dried-up and after awhile I am so stymied I start straying around my stall and poking the books to find the idea. But this is also the blank effort and when I sit down again, I have the same results and I think that if this is only the one letter, the task ahead is going to be impossible to achieve.

And then it flashes over me that I know this feeling like the mama hen knows her chick egg since I used to suffer it all the time when I was struggling to be the notable writer. Ha!, and it's funny to think that I completely forgot about such because long ago composing the right words for my thoughts was the top most important thing in my life. Back then it took up all my mind power, and except for meeting up with the *Ah Nias* now and again, I spent my whole time practicing my words and never playing at what the others were playing or enjoying the frivolous means.

Instead I kept myself purposeful by the grindstone everyday and I lashed myself never to count the hours or watch the weeks until the volume was done, since according to all the notable writers I read, the significant book has no time limit. Until finally I carefully typed my words one last time on the new carbon papers and sent it off to the smart secretary at the literary agency and began picturing my name on the leather spine or even the paper cover, and also how thick this book could be or what the printing can look like. That is, until she returns it right away with only the first pages wrinkled telling me such were read, and attaching the thank you but no thanks note. And so then I tongue-lash myself to make the next edition better and go shut myself away to push my pencil some more and the same thing happens all over.

Throughout the years I did this for four, five, then the half-dozen books. Until one day when just like all my struggling with the *Ah Nias*, I woke up and felt like not performing such anymore. Maybe it was because I got another No thanks letter, or maybe it was that I cannot think of anything notable to say that day. I don't remember how it stopped; could be I just gave up interest in my thoughts. But quick like that it was gone and without even waiting the extra minute, I jam pack all my writings into an old suitcase and bury it under my bedframe where they all have been sleeping since. And next I make up my mind to start my own business and dot dot dot and what have you and the years fly by and I surround myself with all these burdensome books, many of which in my belief should not be circulating, but never once do I think of picking up where I left. And now even though there is only the one letter before me, I am meeting up with this feeling I never thought I would see again, and like before I am at my desk with the scratched out pad and nothing to write and already I am thinking of throwing the towel over what I have begun.

But as I recall all this, it strikes me that instead of hunting my shelfs for the used-up ideas that already were printed I should take a purposeful stroll to inspire my thoughts. Such is the way Mr. Hemingway got his plots I recall, and I think Mr. Dickens, too, though maybe not him so much after he got famous and was harassed by all his friendly admirers. And so locking up Gecko 88, I go down Porridger Road to see the latest occurrences to provide me the good insights, though I am hoping too, that I won't be assaulted by the parade of acquaintances as I am gathering my steam.

And then the strange thing occurs. For even though the hour is not so late, I see that not so many strollers are hasting along on their vital business, or rushing in and out of the eating and drinking places. The newagents are all locked and even the hawker stalls are closing up, and I am wondering what is occurring to the Tandomon econ to make it like this. It is like the whole neighborhood is in the bad mood. And so I am watching the workers put in the new bench for the short-temper tram waiters in front of the Kapoor dental shop when suddenly I glimpse a woman hurrying across the street with the small boy in the school sweater, both dressed like they are fleeing the official function. Because she's tall and her walk is big, the boy is not keeping up so easy and she is scolding him not to be so dragging. But it's when she turns back to proof him that I cognize her as the teacher woman I once spent the whole Sunday afternoon concert with when I was still trying to meet-up the *Ah Nias,* though it was only that time. She's not changed so much but maybe to her I am the different person since she doesn't recall me when she eyes my way and just hurries past. Since I never take photographs of myself I don't know if I'm the same or not.

But that is just the one thing. The other is that as she rushes by, I see the dragging boy's sweater has the big patch with the name of the famous children's school in Tandomon. It is the top-ranking place with all its own books for the pupils so no worrying parents from there ever come into my stall to hunt down volumes for their children's extra drudging. And now even though I still am feeling my surprise from seeing the long-ago *Ah Nia* with her family, glimpsing this patch opens my mind to the new idea that makes me forget all about her and the fancy concert we had and head back right away to Gecko 88. Truth is, I think this *Ah Nia* always was too tall for me.

Once I'm there I double-check my notes and find that just like I believed, Mr. McLemore as the boy attended the Penang Free School in Penang, which likewise is much known here for its traditions and good respectability. All the local peoples praise it like the religious truth, saying that such is where the tree of the future leaders is planted. In fact one *Ang Moh* that used to come into my stall just for the books on ships and trains claimed he also studied there as a boy, although when I read the newspaper story later about this same man getting arrested at the public zoo for throwing off his clothes and aggressing on all the animals there, it nowhere mentioned this prime fact.

But now I'm considering that such a place would be the good beginning for my stories. For one thing, I'm thinking, I can put my father here at the same time as Mr. McLemore and say that they are the longtime friends from then. I can then say my father's father was the keeper of the school grounds and got my father enrolled (otherwise how can he go?), and that he and Mr. McLemore both liked to climb the trees and draw the world maps and catch the flying insects and that's how they got interested with each other. And here's something else...maybe my father and Mr. McLemore also like to read the books by Mr. Kipling and Mr. London and planned to go hunting and exploring the USA when they finished the school. (Ha!, and this is very stretching since my father never dared to pick up any editions except to look at the numbers inside.) And then I can switch up and say yes, but then my father got sick from a local fever and almost got deceased and so skipped some of his sixth form, but Mr. McLemore helped scholar him when he recovered so he could still take his exams. And then after...

And now my thoughts are firing all over the place with these ideas and my black biro cannot fly fast enough to keep up the new twists of my mind. It's like the rain is rushing down the mountain again and very soon I have filled-out my first dispatch to Prof. M. Mittman. But I don't stop there and I go on drafting the even longer list of things to write about since now the ideas are coming one after another like the movie. I compose and compose and don't stop to look until I find that the ink is drying in my biro and that almost all my accountancy book is covered up in my new ideas. In fact it is the entire night I have spent writing these things, I realize, and I am just concluding reading everything over when I glimpse up and see the crack of dawn is arrived and the sun is now looking through my window shades in Gecko 88.

V.

Not long after I send off my arresting letter to Prof. M. Mittman, I am visiting my Cousin Peng downtown where he runs his big newsagents. Cousin Peng is not truly my cousin but we have grown up together since boys and my father was all the time scolding me to keep my eye on him. See, Cousin Peng maybe has the small short circuit or could be the extra wire in his mind, so he lags behind in school until they released him in the upper form. After that he makes his purposeless way here and there until he finds the newspaper business, which he says he likes because he stays on top over how the world goes to bed and wakes up everyday. According to Cousin Peng, this kind of intelligence keeps him sharp with the new outlook. As for me, though, unless I and Cousin Peng are chatting, I keep my distance from the news, which I see as like the fireworks show that just makes the big noises before going away and changing nothing.

But one thing about Cousin Peng. Not like Angry Lim, he's truly longtime married to the beautiful woman. And more than that, this beautiful woman got two eye-picture sisters and they all live together in an old black-and-white on the top of Raiders Hill, which is the most smart area in Tandomon City. Even now I don't know how Cousin Peng performed this miracle feat and despite our years he stays close-mouthed about this stroke, just like the two sisters that I used to try to chin wag but who likewise give me no sway. But from one day to the next, Cousin Peng announced he was marital and that was that. Sometimes when I consider this I think he should be the one looking after me, not the different way around.

Today he starts off like the typical Peng and fills me in on all the matters from his newspapers. The Kwok government is still the shameful sham, he says, and the USA is putting up the new soldier bases in the Indo region and all over the Malay mainland. Then there's a tenement fire that evicted the whole block in Webster Park, and the pack of dogs that yesterday was running up and down Corsair Lane got captured by the city, though three of the officers got scratched up during the dangerous mission. Also the *Ah Soh* that everyone believes was vanished and died only came back from KL where she was visiting her old auntie but failed to tell anyone. Finally, he says, the lottery is up to three-quarters million Tandomon dollars since no one has guessed on the right numbers. Hearing these happenings, the case is proved to me that the world is not so much changed from the last time he informed me.

Cousin Peng then inquires over my doings and here I tell him about the bad state of my bookstall and the volumes that keep piling up, and I wrestle if should mention my letters with Prof. M. Mittman and my new writing. But for the moment I tell myself to stay *tiam*. Maybe I will announce such later when the events are rolling and Prof. M. Mittman's book is completed but until then I don't want to race ahead of myself.

Next though, Cousin Peng inquires over my health situation since this is his chance to fuss me about his black black tea. For some reason Cousin Peng is fixated that I not consume enough of this drink and so he cross-examines me like the barrister each time about do I have enough *Pu-erh* and am I gulping it every night? And no matter that I always reply yes, for every holiday– Ghost Festival, Double Nine Festival, what have you–he presents to me boxes of this black black tea that I then put away on my highest cannot reach shelf since to me it's like drinking dirt. But then comes the next special occasion and Peng turns up again with the new gift box and same speech. He lectures me it's the marvel cure for all things, upper and lower.

So to save trouble I agree once more and we move on to the other topics that are not so pressing for two getting older men. First we grumble about the volumes of Aussie tourists lately coming to Tandomon to buy up the cheap goods and hunt the girls. But after they finish the only thing for them is to drink the Chinese liquor and go provoke trouble, says Cousin Peng and we conform again. Then we consider our old school friend Gao who's trying to defeat the upper hand from time, never mind that he's just leaving the hospital for the arthritis in his joints and bad circulating blood. So now Gao wears a monkey weave hairpiece and the suit of shiny leather clothes and during the day goes plow-plowing down the streets on his loud rumbly Japanese moto-bike so everybody looks. Only thing though, says Cousin Peng, is that the monkey piece flies off no matter how strong the headglue, so Gao has to skid his moto-bike and go pick up his hair before zooming off again. Cousin Peng says he has seen this for himself and shakes his head and once more we have the same mind.

Lastly we chin wag some about the newsagent that got *hoot* up and robbed the other day and that the papers now say could die. In the high daylight, too, with all the law officers around and nobody running down the stealers. Only thing I don't want to be is the obituary, says Cousin Peng mournfully and over such I can see he is positively worried. This I can tell because ever since we were boys, Cousin Peng has the manner of striking the book of matches whenever he grows nervous. So one-by-one he scratches a new light and grounds it out, and does another until the pack is finished up. He does this now as we chat and how he hasn't yet burned down his newsagents or his big black-and-white with the three beautiful sisters inside all these years I don't know.

But anyway, as I am making my goodbye and my mind is mulling over what Cousin Peng has said about the obituaries, it strikes me that if I want to be the valuable book contributor to Prof. M. Mittman I need to know some of the details over how Mr. McLemore got deceased in September 1967. Such is the important piece of knowledge for someone like me to have and I lash myself for not thinking of it until now. So after I leave Cousin Peng I go to the park with the copy of *The Tandomon Talker* he gives me and scan the pages for the dying notices to see the type of facts they like to print. Then I trudge myself back to the Tandomon National Library est. 1914 to find the similar death story for Mr. McLemore.

Like before it's dark and empty inside and even the sleepy looking auntie librarian don't raise up to say anything as I stroll by. But after I stir her she takes me to the special corner room that's got the meat freezer air-con, and stacked up with the plastic rolls of old newspapers all on the film that I have to read on the special machine. The wall is up to the ceiling with such scrolls and because I don't know the first thing about doing the detective search, I poke and hunt and pull down all kinds of publications from all over the world. Scanning such, I think it is like the day-by-day history of everything has got shrunk down inside this room and I wonder what Cousin Peng would say about this.

Because if staying on top of the daily occurrences refreshes the person, what happens when he only knows the past events?

Anyway, it takes some time but finally I find the mash-up of scrolls from 1967. Then because Mr. McLemore is the famous *Who's Who* type of person I take out the A-1 newspapers and rummage them. So now I am spooling through all the editions from Singapore, Malaysia, HK and Thailand for September 1967, which is the drearisome task since there are avalanches of events in these parts the storywriters get worked up about, and soon my eyes are hurting and I'm like ice from the meat air-con. And while plenty of folks choose to fall dead that month, I find no Mr. McLemore. Then checking my watch I see it's almost time to open up Gecko 88 and as the consequence I am ready to forget wanting to know how Mr. McLemore got deceased, or maybe learn the truth another day.

Luckily though I stay at the grindstone a few extra minutes to scour one last scroll, recalling my father who used to scold me to always do the one more thing just when you think you are completed with the task. So for hell of it I decide to look up the local papers and pull out *The Tandomon Talker*. And finally on page number 17 in the Section B on September 9, 1967 below the advert for the pimple liquids, I strike the pay dirt and dig up the urgent account.

Only thing is though, it's not really the obituary for Mr. McLemore, just the regular story with his name written above. It says:

RENOWNED AUTHOR DISCOVERED TO BE DEAD

Resident writer Mr. Lawrence McLemore, who has gone unaccounted for since early June, was discovered perished in a far-off part of Yan Bao sector. The authorities there say the cause of Mr. McLemore's death is unknown but they are sure it is him and that there is no cause for doubt. The touted local author had caused a search to be undertaken after he disappeared in June from the Kong Xie tobacco plantation where he was living. There is no information from the informed sources on the condition in which he was found.

Mr. McLemore had been residing in Yan Bao for several months and apparently got into no previous trouble there, according to the officials, who also say they are regretful about not finding him quicker.

Mr. McLemore's distinguished works include his famous "A Sandwich for Monty" saga, in addition to his early romantic traged-y, "The Smell of Your Memory." His most renowned book, how-ever, is "Potatoes in the Attic", a novel based on his time teaching English to reluctant natives in the Cameron Highlands...

And then the article goes on to inform the details of the death, such as who found him and what time, and there is the blurry picture, too, of the white man with the small mustache that for some reason looks like the Mr. de Gaulle, but now my mind is completely spinning around. Mr. McLemore was deceased in Tan-domon! Ha!, again in this dark empty place I've found the kind of priceless knowledge that maybe no one else knows about and that I also need to furnish Prof. M. Mittman. This is my biggest stroke yet, and again I thank my father who has given the good advice one more time. So forgetting now about Gecko 88, I pull down all the scrolls for all the local papers and begin digging for more prize information. And after scratching in these awhile I root out more clues, even if not everything matches up so corrightly.

For example, the story from *The Tandomon Shouter* says Mr. McLemore's body was discovered by farmers that were shoveling up the village well and it even prints the statement from them saying how Mr. McLemore was dressed all in gray and shaved up like the monk. But then the other piece in *The Tandomon Crier* claims Mr. McLemore got recovered in the morning by the native fishers checking up their traps and it doesn't mention any farmers. And they don't talk about his clothes or haircut, either. And finally, the different one from *The Tandomon Agitator* even states there is too much doubt that the deceased man is Mr. McLemore and concludes the whole affair is one big knocked up hoax and to stay ready for the next story they'll be printing.

But of all these factual accounts, the most significant one is printed in *The Tandomon Bawler*. For the one hand, they declare with no doubt that Mr. McLemore is deceased and they give the name of the important police official that says so. But then they add the burning fact that Mr. McLemore also could be the person who got mixed up in another kind of incident and that such likely was the cause of his deceasement. This type of information is nowhere else in any other story, and what they say is so provoking that after I finish this piece I run to the washroom to rip off the paper towel and come back to copy down all the main parts. The writing that grabs me goes:

Authorities there say they hope the finding of Mr. McLemore, whose well-praised novel, "Potatoes in the Attic" tells the story of a young woman surviving the French Revolution, will not only conclude their months-long search, but also put an end to the many speculations that have surfaced after his vanishing.

Nevertheless, other informed onlookers say that the discovering of Mr. McLemore in such circumstances will only grow the whispering flames of talk that larger intrigues are afoot. These knowledgeable voices say Mr. McLemore's disappearance is greatly similar to

that of Mr. Jim Thompson in the Malaysian highlands earlier this
year, a situation that arose the rumors that Mr. Thompson was a
U.S. intelligence employee. Since Mr. McLemore's disappearance,
the same chatter has circulated from local anti-Communist talkers,
though the British consulate disclaims this to be true. At this point
in time, however, the facts of the case remain very cloudy to all …

How to tell you how these words strike me? Maybe I cannot
express it except to say very profoundly to the bottom of my
feeling. Not so much about the communism or not. That part
doesn't affect me so much since I have always lived in Tandomon,
first for the Japanese army and then the Chinese communists
taking over for the short time later. To me the only governments
that are ever successful at achieving their goals are the ones that
oppress and kill the people. So maybe it's a good thing most governments are failures, I think. No, what stirs me are the words
that Mr. McLemore could be the secret agent working for the
foreign nation. This idea gives me the fierce fierce shock since
for all my life I have been powerfully intrigued by this subject,
second to none. Ever since I was the middle-school boy I was
the bookworm for all the espionage stories, like Mr. Kipling's
Kim and Mr. Maugham's Mr. Ashenden, and later growing-up
the action ones by Mr. Fleming and Mr. le Carré. Even during
my tries at being the notable writer, I composed a few such plots.

Why do I like this type of book so much? For the first thing
these stories always show how the truth of life always stays hidden from the people, and how no one can know about them, only
the danger man. Not only does he have to travel to the far-off
glamorous places for the risky undercover experiences, but in
the end the danger man is the only person that ever gets to know
how the life really operates. People lie to him and he lies back but

he keeps going straight ahead even though he can get found out and killed any time. And then even after he solves the big puzzle, he's got to stay secret over it and pretend the other life while he's still in danger. This to me is the extra big burden since it's one thing to know the real story of the situations but it's the separate matter to stay silent and keep risking oneself. I don't know how the person can achieve this.

But still, even though I devoured these kinds of books always, I never knew anyone who worked at this job since naturally the actual espionage man has to be the underground figure. So learning that Mr. McLemore could be this person gives me the deep jolt; he's not just playing at his books but is the real fact.

Now everything changes for me. Suddenly I no longer care about Mr. McLemore's rubbishy writings. What's more important is his secret life and his danger agent doings. Whenever he traveled throughout the Asian countries, I think he must have seen slews and slews of things and plotted hundreds of intrigues to achieve his goals. Because that is what the real-time espionage man does, not the person who just writes the books to make his living. That kind of *sian* existence is for the others that don't know about the life operations and can only imagine such from newspaper reports. Or who else write the can't-sell books that jam up my shelves at Gecko 88. They are only the actors in the stage show, I think. So to me Mr. McLemore is no longer just the notable writer. Maybe I think, he's like the hero.

VI.

So again that night I use the new facts to fill up the pages of my accountancy book with the vital stories for Prof. M. Mittman. These tales don't come so creatively now since I'm writing about Mr. McLemore's last days, but because I took all the A-1 details from the newspapers for once I don't have to make up everything from the air. Also since now I know this about Mr. McLemore, he is risen in my esteem and I have the real purpose behind my words.

Then for the next few weeks I forget everything about the business of Mr. McLemore and Prof. M. Mittman. Because all of the sudden it's crams time and I am busy raising my cheerful banner, passing out flyers, and ordering up the mug books for all the students to come trudging in with their *kan cheong* parents. This time, though, fewer than ever of them come into my bookstall distressed over their school marks and my volumes pile up all around me. This is a bad sign, I think, and not just for my ledger books. If not so many parents and pupils are terrified over their futures then Tandomon is even worse off than it looks. And so like before, I confirm and double-confirm my figures and play with the plussing and minusing, but in the end they just inform me the same story and now I think that something needs to occur or there will soon be the breaking point. Maybe my twenty years not arrive next July.

Also during this time my friend Charlie O. makes a big decision. He comes in one morning happy like bird and says he's going to Thailand to stay with his friend. And suddenly he looks like the new man that's younger in years, not like my friend Gao who glues on the sham hair and who now I heard walks around lamed from falling off his rumbly Japanese moto-bike. Charlie O.'s face is the real thing and he can't stop himself talking over the future plans he is busy making.

But truth is that while I'm glad for Charlie O., I also have the small pain for myself when I see his change and consider that it comes from the other person. Because this makes me think how I got where I am now. Sometimes I feel like the whole life is just the game of musical chairs and I am always standing when it stops. Or that I am not even allowed to play. But then to boost my thoughts, I tell myself that Charlie O. also is just a little bit older than me and so maybe the game is not yet done for me.

And then the return post arrives from Prof. M. Mittman and suddenly I forget all about my absent customers and missing chairs. Like before this mail comes in the official college envelope but this time it has a home address typed on and it's heavier too, like the professor has discovered more he wants to say:

Delighted to receive your letter. Your stories about your father and McLemore are insightful, entertaining and of enormous help. I feel fortunate to have found such a direct source of knowledge regarding McLemore, not only about his upbringing but also of his adulthood. Already, I have an entirely new perspective on him and his writing.

Okay, I think, I made a good impression with the first stories. This is a relief since it's been a long while since I tasked myself with creating words, especially to a scholar of books. Not anyone can pass such a test of writing, I tell myself.

The professor then says he's glad to know that I'm the successful businessman and he praises me for heading up my important company, though he's also hoping that contributing to his notable book won't eat up the time from my urgent schedules. But because of what I informed him, he says, his book printer already is thinking to double the number of volumes and a local magazine also wants to do the story about his project. My accounts served to bring Mr. McLemore alive to him, he writes, and he looks forward to seeing the next letters.

However Prof. M. Mittman then apologizes for the extra trouble he's bringing me, but he says he's got questions over what I wrote and needs some extra comments about my stories. And here he suddenly makes out the list like he's gone shopping at the night market. For example, can I please provide him the exact times and dates of all the events I described, along with the facts such as peoples' moods, what they were chatting over, why the first place the people got together, and also the weather of such and such a day? Likewise, can I give him any more friendship details between Mr. McLemore and my father, such as what they were like growing up, how their personalities got along and how often they kept in touch since? The professor says he needs to bring out Mr. McLemore's human side in the book or else it will be the failure. In fact, he says, he now is taking the time off from scholaring at his college just so he can be the fulltime writer and he's been working like the bear to research all the vital details he needs.

Now this is a lot of information Prof. M. Mittman jams into the couple short sentences and reading such I get a glimpse of why this man is scholaring at a US college where the students come in everyday to be drilled by the profound things, not like the pupils here in Tandomon who instead want to forget their exams and bypass coming into my bookstall and don't show their faces at the Tandomon National Library est. 1914. This is the powerful impressive message, I think. But at the same time, though, I'm starting to feel *buay tzai* if I can make my level of writing to what the professor wants. If he's this requiring, I consider, I don't want to be like the cannot get it student in the back row just hunching over and praying he will pass. Maybe this coursework is too *cheem* for me and I should drop out.

And in fact almost like he's scanning my mind, at the bottom of the letter, Prof. M. Mittman puts in the last thing to grab my attention. He writes:

P.S.–Again, I just wanted to say how important it is to hear from a childhood friend of McLemore, even if some of these boys' tales sound to me a little "tall" in the telling. Your father's story about their skipping school to go diving from the cliffs, for example, seems rather curious since from everything I know, McLemore was deathly afraid of heights. But I guess that's the job of the lonely biographer, to separate people's fond memories from all the hard facts. But so long as I get lots of both, I'll be fine! Thank you again for your wonderful reminiscences and I look forward to hearing the rest . . .

Okay, I consider. Maybe I extended too far when I wrote the account of how my father and Mr. McLemore would escape classes to go to the mountains and go leaping from the high durian trees into the water. And actually I don't know for facts if the durian grows anywhere on that part of Penang or how far it lies from the school, so maybe I should refrain from such episodes to not stir up the suspicions and be accused of being the big hole. Rather, I think my letters should focus only on the matters Mr. McLemore and I spoke about so no one can question them, and then at the same time put in the whispers about his being the secret agent. That all around is the safer course to keep me out of trouble, I think.

So in my next message I compose the few days later I don't talk so much about my father and Mr. McLemore. Instead I write about how as a boy I was acquainted with Mr. McLemore from my father, and how after he sadly died and I was grown Mr. McLemore and I continued to stay friends. Now I tell all about how Mr. McLemore visits me in Tandomon over the years and I give the stories about his travels and work, and say too about how I started my business and visited Mr. McLemore wherever he lived. I then mention that I also attempted to be the writer before having my successful company, and that Mr. McLemore was the complete generous person to give me his beneficial help and profound insights.

Lastly I talk about some of the crucial adventures we shared, the deep chats we had, and the life advice he gives since I'm the son of his passed-on boyhood friend and Mr. McLemore feels accountable for me. This is something he feels much responsibility for, I say. But at the same time I also drop the inklings about Mr. McLemore being the undercover man, saying that whenever we meet up, Mr. McLemore always has the razor intelligence of the world and usually is more up-to-date about such events than the newspaper accounts. In fact, I say, I am amazed how all the matters he predicts come shortly true. I also add that ever since I know him, Mr. McLemore keeps friends from all sides, from the bank businesspeople to the students at the universities to the top persons in the governments and embassies. He even introduces me to such at the high-class parties he goes to when I visit. No wonder he's such a notable writer, I say, having experiences like these at his fingertips.

And then I cut myself short, even though this is just the iceberg tip of fascinating events I have to keep Prof. M. Mittman entertained and wanting more. Like the time when Mr. McLemore *cabutted* the Chinese Revolution by jumping on the last-second coal train to Haiphong. Or how he kept the butterfly garden at his home in Malaya where he relaxed himself. Or about the old Russia man that used to stay with him for long months but doesn't speak English and Mr. McLemore doesn't know any Russian, either. There are all kinds of urgent details that need to be related about Mr. McLemore when the time comes, I think. Maybe too many to fit in just the one volume.

..*

So weeks fly by again. But this time I don't forget about the writings that I sent off and now am lingering day-by-day to hear from Prof. M. Mittman. But no letters or messages arrive despite my waiting and in the meantime my bookstall also is quiet from the purposeful customers. I think now is my lowest time ever for my business and when my stall rent becomes due, for the first time in twenty years next July I have to walk across the way and lend some from Angry Lim.

Then too, I go visit Cousin Peng again and find out that since the last time we had the talk, he has bought himself a sharp Malay *parang* to carry on his person so he doesn't get *hoot* up and robbed at his newsagents like the one that almost died. This blade is jagged and curved around like a big sharp banana and I tell Cousin Peng not to injure himself since he likes to flash it about. But leaving him, I now think I have another thing to worry myself with.

But then finally the letter from Prof. M. Mittman gets delivered. It still has the Saylorsville college envelope but this time I see there is just the two sheets of writing inside and no home address, only the professor's name printed on the back. Because it's not much to read it takes me only the few moments to scan it over but still I do it twice since sometimes what doesn't get written down is more important than what is there. Such is what I have learned over and over from all the danger man plots.

This time Prof. M. Mittman starts off with the latest news about his book. Since the last letter, he says, the printer confirmed he's going to make the size of the circulating bigger and after that he wants to put in the color pictures, too. He's also special ordering the fancy binding with the dark red leather and then planning to take out the big adverts when it's done.

Now about these matters, Professor M. Mittman trumpets all the details like he's announcing the world news and he even starts to *hao lian* some, though since the professor soon will be the notable writer himself I don't grudge him. I would show exactly the same manner, I think, and maybe inside I am a little proudful also.

The only part I don't understand, though, is when the professor mentions the prestigious foundation that will also be giving him the big award to help finish his writing, since when he gives the name of such I wonder why the company called Ford that makes the automobiles now is interested in the dead notable writers that live in Tandomon. Maybe they are going to name the car model for Mr. McLemore, I consider.

But then Professor M. Mittman gets to the bolts of his message and I learn why his letter is so skinny. The reason is that he wants to say thank you and at the same time that he doesn't need me anymore. The professor says he's glad I contacted him to share my connections with Mr. McLemore but now he's got enough of this kind of material and wants to pay full attention to the serious discussion of Mr. McLemore's writings. Because Mr. McLemore was the highly significant author, he says, his book needs this kind of vital analysis to give it importance. Of course if I want to send him more details he's happy to read such, but he doesn't want to bother me further to dig up these facts and take me away from my urgent work. From now on, he says, I can relax over the subject of Mr. McLemore.

To close up, the professor says that it would give him the great pleasure to meet me one day and that in the future he would like to visit Yan Bao to see where Mr. McLemore was deceased. If that happens, he would surely let me know. In the meantime he sends me his good respects and confirms he'll address me a copy of his book when it gets printed.

Now my mouth hangs and I cannot believe. I want to say back to this letter, How can you refuse to hear more about what Mr. McLemore said to me or any of the exciting stories I wrote down from his life? These events it seems are the most meaningful for his life story. Such as when Mr. McLemore's *sampan* sank and he went swimming across the Mekong to save himself; or when the shady gambler swung the Champagne bottle at him at the Regatta Club; or when he borrowed me the cash after my first business sank into the hole. Even the kind of big guard dogs Mr. McLemore had in Yan Bao is the fascinating fact. All these good accounts can make for the stirring book, especially if the person uses the whispers about Mr. McLemore being the nation's spy.

Now despite his powerful scholar skills, I feel my estimation of Prof. M. Mittman dropping. If he wants to write the book that will grab the peoples' attention he cannot just pile it with the investigations of Mr. McLemore's writings. This kind of book I know from having my bookstall twenty years next July can only get the small peanuts response. Lucky if that type of volume can end up at Gecko 88 marked-down for cheap and then sit on the shelf long years to collect dust before I put it away. I already have too many of these books and whenever someone brings such around to sell me I always have to pretend I don't understand this kind of writing.

But then I realize too, that if Prof. M. Mittman doesn't care for any further stories of Mr. McLemore, my chance to become the most valuable contributor suddenly is dried up. Likely my name now won't even get thanked when the book gets printed and no one will read the things I took the long nights to compose. And so like before, my writing will go *kooning* underneath the rocks and the next time the *South-East Asiatic Literary Review* ticks the local notable writers it can just run the same piece again. This is very bleak, especially since Mr. McLemore is likely the danger spy that the persons should know about. And now it seems again that I have put in all this work only to arrive at the dead end for myself. This blow strikes me hard.

But while I am yet digesting the details of this cruel event, my father's old words suddenly come back to me about how the troubled person never needs to travel mountains for his solution since everything for his problem is at his feet. And so in the difficult situations, he always counsels, one should look first to the ground, not the sky for his way out. Although what this means to me now I am like *sotong*. Right at this moment, I am in Gecko 88 where again no one has entered except the looksee-looksee type that paws everything and carries away nothing, and meantime in front of me there is just the stack of bad news bills the postman has dropped along with the jumble of digests I don't want to look at now. From where can come my answer?

But it's then that underneath this vexing pile I spot a curious item, and so for a few moments stop my worrying to browse the new book that just got left with me. Such is the inches-thick edition by Mr. Hemingway that got found and printed after he died. I'm not so interested to read this due to the scoldings it got from the notable reviewers, but seeing it I am then reminded of the other famous work Mr. Hemingway lost on the train when he was just the starting-off writer and never got discovered. According to the *Indo-Asia Book Journal*, if such writings ever showed up the finder could sell them for many thousands of dollars.

And then in the flash I know right away what I am supposed to do and also all the needed steps I am going to take. It is like the instruction sheet got printed in big type in my mind. First thing, I consider what can happen if any lost writings from Mr. McLemore were discovered. For Prof. M. Mittman, that would be the for-sure fortunate event since not only could he tell the world about such, but he would also be the one to investigate them and declare what he thinks. Besides achieving the acclaim as the discoverer with the big coup, he would suddenly be the big-name person spouting the deep thoughts in all the important journals, with all the official people now wanting to shake his hand and have him at their high-class tables eating their A-1 foods.

Next, I think about what can happen if I owned such writings. If so, Prof. M. Mittman would likely beg to possess these and tell him how I acquired such. I can see him harassing me all day long with his fat envelopes needing to know every new fact over how Mr. McLemore wrote this book, the notable ideas he wanted to discuss, the subjects he talked over with his friends, and my efforts to help him along. And after this there would likely come more fat letters wanting the extra details about these matters, too. Could be that the professor turns out to be the slave driver and I'll be shacked from inventing all these events but if this happens then I am no longer the person Prof. M. Mittman doesn't care to talk to anymore, but his most valuable contributor, for sure.

And finally, here is the last puzzle piece to my thoughts. For even if Mr. McLemore is not so famous like Mr. Hemingway, I think that after Prof. M. Mittman's book circulates there will be the sudden hunger for the new writings by him. It's like when the movie theater tells the people about the coming pictures and all of them show up the next week even if they don't want to care for the film. Most customers, I have learned, usually don't have the idea of what they like unless you give it to them.

Now of course, I am understanding Mr. McLemore's lost book cannot sell for many thousands like Mr. Hemingway's but it won't be chickenfeet, either. For one thing, the local colleges and the Tandomon National Library est. 1914 will pay their attention, and all the literary digests will be glad to scold such a book since the notable writers always are looking out for somebody new to disapprove about. This can fast spread out the word. And then if Prof. M. Mittman becomes the famous USA scholar and Mr. McLemore's book is the bestseller, I could be getting known too, and not just be the growing older man running the *pokkai* bookstall that's lending the rent money from Angry Lim. Maybe then some printer will even ask me for my own book of plots he wants to sell.

So while I'm chewing the news from Prof. M. Mittman that he doesn't want me anymore, all this thinking is flooding my mind. In fact the more I consider, the more my ideas keep spreading and spreading just like the monkey pod branches. So now even though the fresh crowd of browsing customers has just come into my empty bookstall, all I want is for them to go away and leave me alone, please. I got to go busy myself and start writing Mr. McLemore's lost book.

VII.

Whenever I read the stories in the literary digests from the notable writers, there is one matter I cannot figure. Such is how they all claim to forget how they started their writing part of life. *I don't know, I always was writing,* says one; or the other will declare, *Ever since I was the boy I was reading books.* To me this seems like bunkum, like they don't want to sound uppity about who they are now and instead like to say they were once the innocent persons without the cares. Or maybe they don't want to admit they always wanted to be the notable writers. But for me, likely because I am not in their company, I can very clearly recall my starting-off so if someone asks me one day I have the story ready to go. I was just the boy in school but the event sticks to me like yesterday.

In my first year at Slowall Secondary (Ha!, not so much at all like Ansleigh), I was the student in the class of Mr. G. Yeoh for grammars and writing. This was not so enjoyable because Mr. Yeoh was a short man with the roughed-up skin and the tangled-up voice no one listened to. Everyone always did the thing they wanted in his class and he cannot control them ever, even the girls. Likewise, some of the boys were bigger than he so it looked like the comedy whenever he sent them to the headmaster after they acted up and harassed the others.

Then one afternoon almost at the finish of the day, Mr. Yeoh says he wants to read us something and to put away the work. So now we are looking at the clock and counting the minutes until we are released and hoping we do not hear another tiresome lecture about this or that kind of grammar. But Mr. Yeoh takes out a new book his friend has posted him from HK. The title looks to be only for children and already we are making the jokes, but as Mr. Yeoh begins to read the class gradually goes *diam* and everyone starts listening very carefully. The book I recall very clearly is the young adventure story that takes place in England and is named *Swallows and Amazons*, and things happen like the children play at pirates and battle each other and almost fall to death in a lake and search for the treasure and so on, but as Mr. Yeoh reads even the bigger boys that all the time make trouble look much absorbed. When the alarm rings telling us to go home it's like we want to stay and hear more.

So from now on Mr. Yeoh controls the class by saying that if we stop our bad behavior, he will read from the book. Because everyone wants to know what comes next they right away quit their play and nonsense. And then for the half-hour before we leave we listen to Mr. Yeoh read the next part until the book comes to the end and he goes on with another one. All year this goes on and no more problems arise in Mr. Yeoh's grammars class.

At the time this seemed like the powerful magic to me. Mr. Yeoh is short and argly-looking and no one pays attention to him but when he comes out with the story, suddenly everyone kowtows and stays quiet. I am amazed at this, for truth is I'm like Mr. Yeoh. I'm small too, and no one pays attention to me, either; only the bigger boys to hit me and push me down until Cousin Peng who is older by the few years rescues me. (Ha!, and now I consider that maybe Cousin Peng was the trained one to keep the eye on me.) So now I start to think that telling stories is its own kind of power that can spellbind the people, even the enemies, and so I begin creating my first compositions. And from then on I go to the school library everyday and start devouring as many volumes as I can to get my own ideas of what to write and soon I don't care if no one notices me because all the time I have my face in the book.

But here also is when I make a big mistake, even though it takes me years to learn such. For one thing is to enjoy the story, the other one is to be the storywriter. People all the time want to hear the account but when it's finished only a few of them ever think about the person that creates it. But since I want to be the storywriter, I believe that everyone regards him like me. Truth is though, most people don't care who invents them the tale, only how it turns out. So throwing myself into becoming the notable writer is the matter significant only to me and when I tell people my purpose, the result is like before when no one cares to notice.

This knowledge is proven to me many years later when I'm grown up and failed at being the writer and am just starting my bookstall. One day one of the boys that used to push me down comes into Gecko 88 because his beautiful wife is at the high-class dress shop across the way buying her rashes of expensive things. Now he cognizes me right away though I'm not dressed stylo like he since mainly I just pay half the mind to what I am wearing, and also my stall then was small and much crowded for space. But still he sees me and laughs and says, "Po! Still surround yourself with all the books, *lah!*" And then he makes more jokes before he stops to tell me about the topnotch business he runs and the happy children he raised and the Jaguar car sitting outside that he and his beautiful wife are about to drive to the airport to take to their vacation trip. And then like the flash he's gone before I can tell him anything about the significant stories I've read over the years or anything concerning Mr. Hemingway or Mr. Maugham or Mr. Fitzgerald and the works they create or even the books I wrote that now sleep under my bedframe. I just see him looking at me in my jam-pack stall with all the surrounding old volumes and from then on I truly understand how valuable the book person is to others.

However like I said, by the time I learn this piece of wisdom it's too late since as the *Ah Sohs* say, when you spend so many years growing into a thing there is no place else for you in the life.

So it is because I am already in this life that I feel I have the allowance to create Mr. McLemore's lost volume. After all, it cannot be said that I am the imposter after all these years. That person is the one who never attempted the important book or doesn't know anything about the storywriter or how the stories get made. Such a person cannot just think to attempt the other's words.

And besides, how can the beginner person even try to try? This task is no picnic for me, either, since Mr. McLemore's books are filled with the drunk butterfly sentences that are not so easy to copy. I think that because he was likely the danger agent involved in the slew of intriguing matters, how he composes his books is not so important to him.

So I go slowly and it takes me the few weeks before I can create even the smallest chapters. My plot turns out to be about the adventure man that goes off exploring the distant land but gets mixed-up with a bad partner that takes him to the jungle and *kapos* his money and leaves him there to die, only he gets saved by the savage tribe that will kill him anyway, except for the adventure man's friends and also the woman who loves him and comes looking for him, and that then make peace with the tribe and give them medicine dot dot dot and so on. It's like the simple story I read as a boy mixed up with some movie stories I recall, but even still this trifling matter eats up all my blank time when I'm not at Gecko 88 and leaves me much shacked. In fact it goes so slow that I start to worry Prof. M. Mittman will write his book before me and my work will only be the useless attempt. So I think to myself that maybe I should lessen my efforts to a shorter novel, or even the undone piece of the bigger book, for I am also wondering if I can keep up writing in the manner of Mr. McLemore for so many pages.

Meantime though, at least my bookstall no longer is giving me the pounding headaches since all the purposeful customers are doubled back and crowding away the only browsing persons. For fortunate for me, a big typhoon has lately wiped away the villages and scattered the peoples in the areas of Thailand and Malaysia. So the agents have turned around and are now flying the tourists to Tandomon and suddenly everywhere there is the flood of people. Now my bookstall is piled high with the maps and visitors guides and travel books being snapped up *chop chop* by the *Ang Mohs* hungry over where to go and what they want to see right away. Cousin Peng gives me extra copies of his newspapers and these sell out, too, and even my volumes of Mr. Robbins and Mr. Sheldon get shopped so I can finally rid myself of these rubbishy writings. And for the first time in the long while I can breathe with more relief and don't go to sleep with my accountancy books preying my mind.

But it's in the middle of these full plate times that I also get the surprise letter from Prof. M. Mittman. At first when I see it mailed so quick, I feel *kan cheong* like the professor has scoured my facts and wants to double-interrogate me over this or that crucial detail. But thankfully this is not so. Instead after regretting himself for disturbing my urgent business, the professor says he has just the two questions, if I can answer please. The first is not the big deal and is over the whatnot matter of when this particular event takes place between Mr. McLemore and my father. He says he doesn't know if I am saying nine o'clock at night or in the morning in my letter and can I clear up? So I read that and think, Ha!, so maybe something I created still is left in his important book and my contributions are not the lost cause. Could be I underestimated my vital efforts.

However, Prof. M. Mittman's second request then gives me the bigger concern and now I go speechless in my mind since it's like the professor has again taken out his X-ray machine to scan inside my thoughts. Because now Prof. M. Mittman is asking do I know anything about any leftover writings Mr. McLemore might have composed? That is, did Mr. McLemore ever say anything about what he was writing on before he died, or did I know what happened to any of his important papers after he was deceased? He's investigating if there's something new he can use for his book.

Of course, Prof. Mittman is just acting the nosey parker but reading such I still get a fluster of how does he know this, and now I am seriously wondering if he has the information that can *la sai* for me. Or if there is the grave matter I am blur to and am going to accuse myself of. And so my cautious mind says to read the letter twice and maybe endeavor myself to cow down my efforts.

But that only lasts the moment. For then I realize that Prof. M. Mittman's letter is actually the gold situation, especially since the professor has become the eager asker. Now I can skip my kowtowing to convince him Mr. McLemore had these leftover writings and my worry that this story can be believable. In fact, my anxiousness now changes to that Prof. M. Mitman will want to see these pages right away and I'll be hammered to invent the good plots. And because I'm already slaving for the inch-to-inch progress, this can make for the boiling point.

So contemplating this in my thoughtful manner, I take out my biro and begin penning the long reply that I think I will post in several weeks. For I am calculating that when I receive Prof. M. Mittman's answer to this letter, and then delay to write again, two months can slowly pass. And then I can blame the Tandomon delivery for extra weeks. And this I consider will give me enough of the breathing space to write the urgent stories for Mr. McLemore's lost book.

So in the leisurely way, I say to the professor, Hello, nice to hear from you and I clear up the whatnot matter of the nine o'clock. I then say Yes, I often visited Mr. McLemore over the years in Yan Bao where he kept the very solid English-type bungalow with all the staff servants, and where we would drink our teas and have our stirring talks over the many gripping topics. Next I give the details of this place, how comfortable it was and all the foreign visitors that Mr. McLemore used to receive there, along with their habits and manners. I even say there was such the orgy of persons from all the walks of life there got spread the whispers Mr. McLemore could be the Western agent. Of course I add this is nothing but the talk cock and for him not to pay attention.

And then I drop my explosion. For next I say that because I was the frequent guest at Mr. McLemore's house in Yan Bao, after he died I did get the phone call once from the faithful servant there. According to this old butler, there was the last box of Mr. McLemore's important possessions they don't know what to do with. The police don't want and since Mr. McLemore is not survived by anyone they say they may have to toss such away. Can I please advise?

It's when I hear this, I say, that I journey up to the plantation and find the small piece of writing that I believe is Mr. McLemore's last work. It's in the mash-up of his other papers

but truly looks like the final story he was assembling. The title
of this I recall is *The Traders* and I give some of the plot of the
book I am writing. And here I create the adventuresome good
idea to say that this piece of lost writing was finally buried by Mr.
McLemore's butlers there as the last tribute.

Then I stop my letter since like before I do not want to spill all
my fascinating beans at once. When the time comes I think I will
next describe how I recently drove up to Yan Bao during the big
storm and after much haywiring and confusion dug up the book
under the hundred-year-old lime-bird tree that looks over the
river. This kind of event can give my story more of the venturesome that I feel the professor would want to devour.

So keeping the don't care manner, I say goodbye to Prof. M.
Mittman and ask if this is the kind of particular event he means
and does he want any more details of such? And then I wait for
three weeks and I post my letter.

Not long after that, I am in Gecko 88 one morning when the
young boy pedals up to give me the breathless delivery. At first
I don't know what he is handing me since never before in my
life have I got the telegram and never have I received any since,
though I glimpsed it lots of times in the movies like when the
girl gets the notice her soldier man dies, or when the famous
explorer tells the newspaper that he made it safe to that part of
the world. Sometimes too, the bank loses the money and so the
family has to move or the man jumps from the building. Always
it seems the music plays louder and everyone holds their breath
or is waiting to cry out since this is the most urgent moment they
have been waiting on.

This moment though is not like any of that. Instead my telegram is from Prof. M. Mittman and is only several sentences long
and even if the music was swelling or the family was wailing I

don't think I could hear such. For all the sudden I am stopped in my cold tracks by Prof. M. Mittman's telling me that my finding of Mr. McLemore's lost book is the great and exceptional news for which he cannot ever thank me enough and cannot ever profoundly repay. He is beyond fortunate to have found me, he says, and maybe for this he should thank the god. But my news is so exceptional that after hearing such, he right away has bought the ticket to Tandomon to come see this writing and so as the result he looks forward very much to meeting me in the next few days.

VIII.

Now unfortunately this isn't the only terrible news that Prof. M. Mittman unleashes on me in his small writing. After he informs me of his arriving, the professor then says he'll be bringing the person that's making the TV report over Mr. McLemore's lost book and who wants to interview my thoughts too, because my personal acquaintanceship with Mr. McLemore also is the key heart of the story. Also, since the film of him finding these writings will be the powerful event, he wants me to deliver him to Yan Bao to discover them. There are other details, too, the professor says, but he'll tell me when he sees me at the address on my letters since whenever he tries to long-distance me, the operators cannot find the number for my company. And then there is the See you soon and Goodbye.

Now here is the funny thing. Despite all the bedlam roaring around me, the only thing I can think of for some reason is the old-time radio song about the girl with her parade of cheating boyfriends, and who sang that her troubles always travel in the big, medium and small size, just like the family. This was the long-ago popular tune called *Don't Grief Me Up (With Your Troubles Anymore)* and was so favored for awhile that when Tandomon became its own sovereign, the leaders almost made it the national song. But then it got discovered that the melody was partway written by a communist Chinese man who dictated over the people there and so to support those persons' freedom the Tandomon leaders banned the music off the radio and outlawed to play it and made another song the country anthem. Fortunate for herself, the singer had tragically died by then and so avoided the jail term for singing such.

Now I have not thought of this melody for many years but after Prof. M. Mittman's terrible note, I suddenly am considering this song's message and wondering how does the person know which size news he is getting when he is trapped in the storm of ugly events? For sometimes the small matters become worse over the days, and other times the worse things show a lesser face the longer they go on. Because suffice my saying, at this present moment I am feeling like the besieged person on every side.

For one thing, the tourists that had been cramming my shop just yesterday now are passing it by since all the sudden the *siong* hawkers are sprung up all over selling their own maps and travelers books. Up and down Porridger Road there are propped-up stands and some even pitched the camps at the airport to barrage the visitors as they come trudging off the jets. Now my books are piling up around me again and no one comes inside to look at the discounts I am special offering and once more I am thinking maybe I have to go to Angry Lim.

Then too, Charlie O. no longer is leaving off to Thailand since he and his friend had the big fight and broke up completely and don't want to speak anymore. This is an extra-sad case and now Charlie O. stops by every morning before I open my stall and repeats to me his story even though I can only reply him with the same handful of no use sayings that he doesn't want to hear, anyway. And so the next day is the replay of the one before and when

I listen to Charlie O. I began to wonder if this kind of relationship is worth it if the person needs to suffer like that in the end.

And now even Cousin Peng is in trouble for waving around his *parang* in the dangerous manner. On his side, Cousin Peng says he was being threateningly attacked and almost robbed at his newsagents but the Tandomon officials that give him the summons instead say that Cousin Peng was terrorizing the *Ang Moh* tourist from Europe that can't see so good and only wanted to buy the chocolate bar from Horlan. Either way, Cousin Peng has to go sell off his family's valuable tea chest to pay the barrister to talk for him in court and settle his fine and after this Cousin Peng's beautiful wife doesn't speak anything to him for the entire week. The police also take away his *parang* and put Cousin Peng's name on the list of people who cannot have such ever again.

And then there is the last matter for me, which is that Mr. McLemore's lost book is still the heavy load and during this time I can only create the slim volume of pages. Even though I drudge with patience and keep drinking my *kopi-o*, after the long night I have just the handful of worthy sentences. Over and over I try to set myself in the mind of the danger agent like Mr. McLemore to create the intrigues that have happened but my words always plow to the complete halt and now I am thinking that Mr. McLemore's lost work can end up being only the short story.

And so now because I am beset by all the sides there is nothing for me to do except take the counsel again from my passed-on father and keep calm and suffer my hardships straight-on. Nobody likes to watch the panicking man sweat, he used to advise, before repeating the story of the *kuat* tree-cutter man in the old Tandomon folk tale. (Of course this tree-cutter man also got torn up by the forest dragon because he kept the silent attitude but this part I try not to linger on.) So the day the professor says he is supposed to come and meet me and all the next one too, I put on the extra-serious face whenever the new customers enter and I take the pains to wear my better clothes so I don't look like the tumble-down man who runs it. I even try to pen some last pages for Mr. McLemore's book but this remains the difficult chore.

It takes until almost the end of the second day before the professor finally shows himself. Right away I can tell it's Prof. M. Mittman because he doesn't stride in like the customer that's going to paw the shelves searching for the cheap book but instead checks the surroundings in front, then double-confirms the paper in his hand and glimpses over my bookstall before he enters. And once he's inside he hunts around some more before coming to talk to me.

—Excuse me, he says in a big voice like the ship's horn. I'm here to see Mr. Po.

Now this person does not fit my bill by any means of what I think he should be like. I am the short man to be sure, but this guy is a large one, even for the *Ang Mohs* that mainly are taller than the Asian persons. I think Prof. M. Mittman has got to be more than six feet and he's full all around like an *Ah Pooi*. His red hair is curling on the sides though not so much on top for the younger man, and he's wearing the short boy pants and tight shirt over the stomach that is sticking out like the kitchen shelf and there's a shiny gold watch on his arm. Maybe too, he's not adjusted himself yet on how to walk here because he's also sweating pools like he just came out from the shower and his bushy beard is dripping also.

But because I'm in the bookstall business twenty years next July and have glimpsed all of the kinds of customers, I just return him the steady look.

—Yes, I say in my firm voice. I'm Po.

Now his face changes from the hunting one to the serious look and he reaches over his big hand to introduce himself. I'm Doctor Mittman, he says, and now he's gripping me with big fingers wet like a dishrag and that don't let go while he's telling me how pleased he is to see me and thanking me for the help I gave him so far. All the material I provided has shown him the deeper insight on Mr. McLemore, he says, and is even more valuable since it is something no one else can furnish. On and on he goes with his thankful speech until finally he releases me and I can pull out the chair for him and sit back down and wipe off my hand.

Under my light, I then take the closer glance at the professor. From his letters I pictured the American scholar as not being so different from the Asian one but instead this Prof. M. Mittman recalls to me the joking man I sometimes see on television selling the house soaps or personal products. He's got a long face like a breadloaf and big white teeth that he likes to show off when he speaks, but his eyes are also round like coins and his nose is shaped like the beak so when it twitches it moves the whole side of his face alongside like he's wearing a rubber mask. He doesn't change his voice so much either, so even though he looks happy now I think he secretly might be the *ngeow* type of man who goes around unpleased over everything and is ready to complain at the hat drop about all the small matters.

Now even though we start off chin wagging pleasantly over the whatnot things, right away I clear up the confusion and tell Prof. M. Mittman that this stall is not my real business and that I keep the address only for my big company's tax purpose. When the collection man comes around, I say, he sees I have the losing operation and my business is not smacked so hard. The truthful place of my ventures is in downtown and today I'm just waiting for my shop boss who had to run his wife to the neck doctor.

—That's a smart thing to do, the professor replies and he takes the look around before confirming himself his statement. That's a very smart thing. The collectors must be like sharks here. Really, who could make a living selling used books? Who'd want to do that?

Of course, the professor doesn't want to be insulting and I cannot be angry over his comments since I am also guilty of disguising my truths from him, but when Prof. M. Mittman says this I still feel a big lash of irritation. How does he know about the business I started twenty years next July? I am thinking. These are books, man!, and it's only because of them that he has arrived here from across the world and is sitting to hear the crucial things I have to say to him. To my mind, he should show the respect since we are both in the same trade.

But Prof. M. Mittman goes on like it's not so important since after all it's only the kind of joke the *ngeow* person would make anyway, and so he changes the subject to inform me fully about his significant project and the important people that's involved in it. First he mentions the Ford money that's buying his trip, then the college scholars and book printers that's excited for him, and also the TV person making the story, and don't forget the magazine writer, either, and as he continues on it sounds like everyone in the USA is in the big lather over his project. And hearing such my biting worry comes back to attack me.

The only thing snagged up, he finally says, is that the camera person cannot yet leave the country and still has not arrived over. But this can likely get untangled soon and everything will then be the action.

To all this, I nod and say not much and try to stifle down my worrisome feelings. But holding off my anxiousness brings up another feeling I also don't want to experience now. For truth is, the longer Prof. M. Mittman proclaims about his significant work and everyone that's esteeming him, the more I'm growing the disfavor of him. It seems there is no room to talk edgewise about anything except his achievements, even to ask the questions about myself. And the more he touts himself, the more his nose twitches on his rubber face like he's preparing another long list of praises in his head, and the bigger his eyes grow like he's only just started lecturing me. Truth is, this man reminds of the always correcting teacher the students dread to have, the one who slaps your hand if the cursive goes over the rule line or if you don't know the Tandomon presidents in the right order. Surviving such is always the difficult chore until the next year, I recall. To nudge Prof. M. Mittman back on the other path then I wait until he takes the breath and ask that since he's the scholar of English, what category of books is his favorite to read?

This makes the professor stop his story about the printer begging to tear up his contract to make him one for more money and his face suddenly darkens like I mentioned the religious sin. He then takes out a set of glasses thick like telescopes and arranges them high up his beak nose before resuming himself.

—I don't read books, he says in the sharp voice. I study texts. I teach textual analysis.

Now this is the new one for me but the way Prof. M. Mittman declares it, it's like the fact I should already know. Of course, I haven't talked with a college teacher since I quitted school during the war and never returned but still I crammed two years of history and literatures at the Tandomon Junior Institute of More Studies ("*Life is Short, Dare to Suffer*") and even mug some Japanese when Tandomon was occupied, so I have a little knowledge. But I never heard once about this field.

Politely I ask him what he means by analyzing texts.

—My background is in textual annihilation, he says. I'm a textual annihilatist. My work has been with Dr. Mullock at the Piish

Institute. Annihilatively speaking, we don't read texts since we believe that the writer's words corrupt the innate harmonization of literary impulse and are pointless to our larger understanding of them. What we address instead is pre-cognitive intentionality, so our work tries to analyze what the writer did before he changed his mind. That is, what the author *might* have written. This to us reveals the true nature of the text.

I am not understanding the single word this man says but am fighting hard to keep my expression set, just like the blur student has to do so he doesn't get hit or left behind by the *cher*. The three or four customers browsing my stall now are also glimpsing at the professor with the same worrisome look. Meantime however, Prof. M. Mittman keeps rolling on with his essay.

—In. T.A., we maintain our distance from books so we can perceive them more fully, he says. The premise of T.A. is that our lack of knowledge in the midst of our inquiry is what leads to real comprehension. To take an example, does the cow grazing with the others in the field know it's a cow or does it view itself merely as part of the overall herd? What does the proximity of other bovinity have to do with its understanding of itself? Is it more a cow or less of one if it grasps its pre-cognitive identity? These are the kinds of essential questions that lie at the heart of our approach. But to answer your question: no, I don't *read* books.

Now I still am catching no ball from the professor's mouthful and some of me also is wondering if I made the mistake and Prof. M. Mittman is the scholar of farming, not books. But since all my browsing customers now have been chased away by the professor's speech, I go ahead and ask him, anyway, How does one know about the books without reading any of the words?

—We review synopses of texts prepared by encapsulators who study the day-to-day habits of authors and are certified in their assumptive capabilities, he says. Some of these synopses are quite detailed but in no way do they reference the actual text. In this manner, we can analyze the works on their most atomic terms without being influenced by their contents. I myself am a credentialed authority on five Western authors, including Lawrence, Dreiser, and the Old Norse poet, Mims Urinis, although to keep my certification I'm careful never to read any of their works, only the most circumjacent summaries. Of course, sometimes actual readers do crop up among the encapsulators and respond to the books' contents, but with the greater formalization of annihilative practices, they've mostly been screened out and the outside influences are becoming rarer. Ours is a very rigorous analysis.

Now this really sounds like the whole bunkum to me, like the professor is just *ji siao* me and waiting to finish the joke. Hard enough to know sometimes what writers mean even when one does scan the words, I think. The professor must see what kind of fish look crosses my face because he goes on.

—Dr. Mullock is the leading textual annihilator in the field, he says in his cutting voice. Of the five people in the world who understand his work, two were at Piish. I feel extremely fortunate to have been his student.

And then he gives me the exact pitying look that the *char tau* student in the far row gets when he doesn't catch on after many tries.

Fortunate for my expression, though, my phone starts ringing and I got to hurry off to address the customer that's trying to narrow me down if I got this or that book advising what to do when your man leaves you for the other woman, and then how to get him back. And so when I return Prof. M, Mittman looks like he has forgotten his lecture and instead is writing his thoughts with a silver biro in his yellow pad. His red face is scrunched up like a worrying tomato and he doesn't look up again until he's done scratching down his important passage to himself.

—I'm very glad we've met, he says when he's finished and sticks away his pages. I have a feeling we're on the verge of some very important work. McLemore's manuscript I imagine is just brilliance. I just knew he had some unpublished writing. When can we start? Is tomorrow too soon?

Now even though this catches me by surprise, I manage to do the quick thinking and say that unfortunately such a day is taken up for me, making the professor let out the *mah fan* sigh like this is the big bother that no one can fix. But then he fires back what about the day after, and to this I find myself nodding yes, that is acceptable. Prof. M. Mittman then considers and says maybe this is better since then the camera person can arrive to take the film of the interview at my company office. Such will look more official, he says, and be better for the television.

Now maybe I nod and say this is all right, too; could be I don't. Mostly I am just feeling the daze. However to his mind Prof. M. Mittman is all agreed and so he grabs my hand with his sweaty rag fingers and doesn't let go again.

—Perfect, he says in his horn voice. You can show me around your company and we can have our discussion there. I have a thousand questions I want to ask you, but not here. Truthfully, this kind of setting always depresses me. I really don't like to talk about writing surrounded by all these old books.

IX.

Fortunately because Tandomon is yet the small type of nation, every person is still close-by connected with all the others, like that gloomy *Ah Chek* with the half past six repair shop, or that old *Ah Beng* married to the skinny *char bor* with the chicken rice hawker stall, or the *lao chio* widow who teaches the nursery school. So when Prof. M. Mittman tells me he's staying at the Heaven View House, I know right away that the cousin of Angry Lim's chicken leg half-sister is the one bossing it. Big Yoshi who I met the once or twice is the Chinese Japanese man who likes to drink *arak* and play at beetle fighting and mostly leaves the business to the Malay *ger* he married. Angry Lim says he's always mostly friendly except when his beetle loses the match.

Likewise, because I spend my entire life yet in Tandomon I also know that Heaven View is not really a hotel most of the time, just when the tourists arrive. The rest of the time Heaven View is really the charnel house since mainly the Tandomon visitors are far between or only come by accident. But times like now when the tourists are flooding, Big Yoshi shuts off the downstairs room for the bodies, then opens the rest for the staying people and he turns around the sign out front so it says *Hotel* not *Beloved Interments*. Over the years he does this, Big Yoshi says the only problem ever occurred was when the drunk tourist once returned late past midnight and accidentally broke into the dead persons room to sleep. After he woke up, the man got hospitalized for two months with bad dreams, he says.

I am recalling all this as I'm riding in the taxi to snatch up Prof. M. Mittman so we can have our serious talk over Mr. McLemore. For this crucial investigation, I have dug out my special white suit with the extra double pleats that I bought many years ago and which now is even looser on me (Ha, I am still the slim man!), and which is not yet so out-of-style, even if the smell is moth flakes. The taxi man wrinkles his nose when I get in the cab but I don't fire back any words to him since all the drivers now are busy with the tourists and I am lucky for his ride.

But another reason I *kek sai* him is that I don't want any other worries preying my mind since I am consumed with anxiousness over the scenes that are about to be played. Because I had only the one day to arrange such matters, I asked Charlie O. to lend his ex-friend's office for the place to meet up Prof. M. Mittman. And since Charlie O. is still angry at the ex-friend, he gave me the keys and said I'm welcome to take anything I want. He also promised to tear the business name off the doors and cover the Tandomon flag over it. He says it serves his ex-friend right and I am thankful to have such the faithful person as Charlie O.

So now we have come to Big Yoshi's hotel that is busy with the tourists pouring in and out the doors and I can already see that Prof. M. Mittman is not being the patient man, but waiting in front with the sweat dripping from his *ngeow* face and holding the cheap rucksack like the kind they sell at the souvenir places. Like me, he looks like he's in the *bin chow chow* mood, and in fact the moment he climbs into the cab he already is complaining over the camera person that still cannot leave the USA and so there will be no film today, only the tape recording. And then he goes on a long growl about how terrible the USA officials are now and how the place overall there is going to hell.

As for me, I reply Okay, too bad, and such is regrettable to me, too, and I put on my disappointed look. But truth is I am much relieved since all along I was worrying myself about being in the TV show that will play in the foreign country. One thing is to be the book expert in Tandomon and the other is to be that person in the USA where many such people are. I would not like to receive the overseas telephone call accusing me of being this or that false thing, and then worry if the others will follow up to plague me. So as we drive along and Prof. M. Mittman and I chin wag over the usual tourist things, I feel myself relaxing and hear my words slipping off my tongue like I'm already performing my interview. And so when the professor all the sudden asks why my company is the one that's open on the Saturday, I smoothly say that according to the national law every fourth Saturday is the business day in Tandomon, and I keep my plain face on even when the taxi driver gives me his look in his mirror. And after that the professor stays silent and just stares out the window until we arrive at the place.

Now Charlie O.'s ex-friend is the big importer for women's clothes and has the offices in the smart downtown area, although of course everything now is empty of people and I'm hoping Prof. M. Mittman doesn't see this fact. But like Charlie O. pledged, the Tandomon flag is draping from the company door and when I enter in my white suit with the extra double pleats, the air-con is roaring full-blast and I can hear noises from the meeting room like the urgent business conference is in the middle. So far so good, I think, and even though it is his misfortune that has provided it, I again give my silent thanks to Charlie O. For now I am going to let Prof. M. Mittman glimpse the important meeting that is occurring so he can rest assured over my company and believe the details I am about to inform him.

Leading the professor to the conference room, I then say to him in the low voice, Board directors meeting!, and then step aside and pry the door so he can get the peek of the meaningful doings.

And there like I planned everyone is seated around the big executive table looking like they are deeply involved over chewing the profits for this or that month, or arguing whether to fire such and such switch-off worker. Such was not so easy to arrange only on the one day and for the moment I am feeling proud over what a simple bookstall man can pull off. (Ha!, not gone case yet!) But when I swing the door wider, I see on the second glance that the setting is not the picture I hoped. For instead of the official persons doing the vital talks, there is Angry Lim snoring with his one eye open; Charlie O. in the corner bawling over his ex-friend; and Cousin Peng beside him lighting and snuffing out his matches. And rather than the crucial documents scattered on the tables and the briefcases on the chairs, the room is nothing but the persons crying and wheezing in the big cloud of match smoke, with the snack foods spread all over, too, and no one even looks when I crack the door. Overall the scene is more like the hospital waiting area for the about to die patients instead of the powerful executive room, and so pulling quickly on the professor's sweaty arm, I slam the door, grumble some low words and start hustling him down to the office of Charlie O.'s ex-friend to make him forget this image. Since Prof. M. Mittman is the *Ah Pooi* man, I can hear him huffing as we haste across the carpet and I am hoping that if we rush ourselves along, this can prevent him from speaking up with his questions. Furthermore, as I twist the key in the lock I also am hoping the ex-friend has got the beautiful view of the downtown buildings–and not the garbage boats sitting in the water–so the professor can study this impression and fully dismiss the persons bawling and snoring.

—This is my office, I say and we go in.

But here again is another bad disaster and this time there is no way to escape such. Because Charlie O.'s ex-friend is the seller of women's clothes, I see his executive office is not like the regular person's; instead this room is full up with the naked woman dummies all wearing nothing but the red panties and black bras, though some only got on one or the other, and a few have no clothes, only the wigs. Some of these panties and bras also are on the chairs and tables, and one bench has the two naked women by themselves laying down on top of each other. On the desk meantime, there is the tall close-up photograph of Charlie O. with his face looking like he's about to give the big kiss.

Now here is something funny about the people from the USA Usually most of them like to talk about all kinds of matters to whoever they meet, even the strangers on the street. It's important for them to be cheerful in any situation, I think. Such is not like the Tandomon persons that only discuss their things after the long time of acquaintance. And even then the person likely can only get half the story.

But sometimes too, depending on the topics, the American people can be the opposite and hold back their tongues. Usually this is when there are the religious or sexual subjects involved, and in that case it is like the thing is not existing for them and is shameful to think about, even if it's right before them. A long time back, my school friend had a beautiful *anoneh* girlfriend and he told me the Japanese persons can be like that too, although they usually are doing so to be first-class polite and not so much worried over the occurrence in question.

So fortunate for me this is one of those times. Even though I can see Prof. M. Mittman is trying not to think about why the executive president of the A-1 trading and development company has the grown-up naked dolls and the women's red underwear inside his office to show the stranger, like the person with the blind eye he just takes the black bras off the chair and doesn't say the word to me. Likewise I go sit behind the desk and don't talk either, though when the professor starts digging in his cheap pack for his items, I turn down the tall photograph of Charlie O. and sweep the panties off my desk. And I keep quiet some more until Prof. M. Mittman lugs out his tape recorder and gives me the okay nod.

—I think we're ready, he says and though his scholar expression is like it was before, maybe his voice is a little bit changed from the minute ago when I was just the regular person in the white suit and not the one having this kind of room.

I nod back and reply that's fine with me. The professor then makes the long note to himself on his yellow pad.

—Good, he says. I'd like to begin with some questions about McLemore's everyday life. I'm analyzing his work using Quotidian Theory, which studies the habits and thoughts of writers when they're not writing, which essentially is when they are their most creative. Quotidian analysis examines how they perform their most mundane tasks and errands, the activities they enjoy and the ones they dislike, and the daily matters that preoccupy them. How they navigate their social realities, so to speak. Since you were a good friend to McLemore for many years, I'd like to ask you some things about this part of his life.

Now when the professor unloads this on me suddenly I am feeling like I'm back in my bookstall when I was the blur student catching no ball from his speech. Even though all last night I mugged the long list of intriguing recollections of Mr. McLemore to deliver, now I feel like I crammed all the wrong subjects. What does the professor mean about the social realities? Is he saying he doesn't want my stories, like when Mr. McLemore got thrown from the fancy Bangkok restaurant for insulting the Viet general? Or when he saved the import-export man with only the one hand from fighting the communists but who lost his house at the *pai gow* table and so had to leave the country until Mr. McLemore pulled the string? Are these kinds of details not big enough for Prof. M. Mittman's book or is he not believing me and maybe trying to catch me in the fraudulence? Looking at his breadloaf face, I am getting not the clue. So going slow with my words I ask carefully if he is talking about the kind of theory he studied in school, the one where the scholars stay away from the writers' writings.

—Well, Q.A. isn't as rigorous as T.A., the professor says with the laugh like he's admitting the fault. And it can involve some reading of the author's work and that is one of its main criticisms. But the fundamental principle is the same, which is that only by divorcing ourselves from the actual writing can we understand at all what the writer is trying to say. As a result, Q.A. focuses on the routines, the thoughts, even the simplest opinions of the writers themselves. For example, did McLemore ever tell you what brands of shirts he liked, or what types of TV shows he watched, or even his thoughts on the local news? Through Q.A., for example, I'm firmly of the belief that even though none of his writings touch upon the subject of colonialism, McLemore was a bitter anti-imperialist whose books all take this as their implicit topic and thus refract and give context to his personal conflict over being both the observer and participant in such a world historical event.

Now I am stumped even more since what Mr. McLemore might have thought of the local affairs I cannot guess, even if he was the undercover man. Truth is, when it comes to such matters I think most people believe that the less is argued over and the more is forgot about, the better. Although I think too, that if the local leaders spent more time reading the good literary works instead of making speeches over why they should be leading, maybe there would not be so many matters to forget about originally.

Then too, I am feeling that the longer Prof. M. Mittman speaks his theory, the more he'll just turn into the statement machine squawking the bird language of scholar phrases. And that if I answer back, all his *kong chiao weh* will only get louder like a big echo chamber repeating the mixed-up noises. If that were to happen, I am thinking, then for sure I will be suffering my pounding headaches again and everyone is just at the square one with nothing gained.

So instead of replying I just wait myself to see what he wants to know. Part of me now is wondering if Prof. M. Mittman really plowed any of the drudging books by Mr. McLemore to get his conclusions, while another half is considering if maybe our discussion is already over and I said too much. But then the professor reaches over and puts his tape machine on the desk by Charlie O.'s picture.

—So let's start by discussing McLemore's day-to-day habits, the things you personally witnessed, he says. This is at the heart of my analysis. You were his guest many times in your life... can you describe some of his everyday routines? For example, did McLemore go to bed late, was he an early riser? Did he like to sleep in?

This I can easily reply to so I state right away.

—He woke up early, I say. Around seven o'clock, sometimes later. And he always liked to sleep by midnight.

—Good, says the professor. That's very important. That matches my understanding of the auroral quality of his mytheme. Rarely, in my opinion, is McLemore's narreme caliginously connotational. And on the occasions where it is, it's hard to escape the sense that it's an ironical usage. Now based on this, do you remember if McLemore bathed in the morning or at night?

—Ablutions in the morning, I say decisively.

—Shave everyday?

—Always, I say and nod strongly.

—Good, I also get that impression from his work. At times, the intensity of his pilosity is overwhelming. Now, did McLemore read his newspapers before breakfast or during?

—After breakfast, I say. He never liked to mix words with his food.

—Ah, that's most intriguing, says Prof. M. Mittman, his voice rising up a notch. And again, perfectly in keeping. From my study, McLemore always took care to maintain the distinction between his naturist sentiments and his post-nominalistic ones. Very important for him. All right then, what did he usually drink with breakfast, coffee or tea?

—All the time coffee.

—Ha, exactly right! Just what I thought! exclaims the professor. Exactly what I thought! Rejecting the imperialists' jentacular potables for the native beverology! This comes through clear as day in book after book. He always was adamant on this point. Now did he take it with milk or sugar?

—Both of them, I say. He liked the sweets.

—Naturally, says Prof. M. Mittman who then writes this down with a grave face and his biro scratching the yellow sheets like he's started on the long essay, even if from my upside-down watching it just looks like lots of duck marks with a drawing every once in a while of a rice pot. Overall he finishes up four big pages until he closes his pen and looks up again. And now I see his face is trembling with the powerful exertions and he starts speaking in a low voice like we're in the Christ church.

—This brings me to the very heart of my study and the one matter that has always been controversial in regards to McLemore's work, he says. I believe it defines the entire epistemology of his writing and so I feel extremely fortunate to be speaking with someone of such an important stature who has witnessed firsthand his métier.

I nod and agree to this about myself.

—You were McLemore's trusted friend and guest throughout the years, says the professor. You've sat with him countless times in the morning exchanging your views, thoughts and conversation. I imagine you've seen him in every imaginable situation from middle age onward... I can't imagine a better person to ask this question to settle this issue. Tell me... what did McLemore have for breakfast?

I act for a moment like I'm recalling the most difficult fact from the deepest earth.

—I remember his breakfast always started with the juice and toast, I slowly say.

—Yes, yes, I thought so! Prof. M. Mittman now starts shouting at me and his face is all lit up. Toast is the major theme in all his writing! It displays fully his feelings over colonialism and his contempt for the imperialist order. It's the burning of innocence. Is nothing so innocent as bread?

—Then what? he asks anxiously after he calms down.

I think hard some more and go back into the earth.

—Then he would have the strawberry jam, I say.

The professor's coin eyes get bigger.

—No! The blood of the conquered!

—Except sometimes... I say, then stop. I can see Prof. M. Mittman is quivering now like the big balloon ready to pop.

—Except sometimes...?

—Sometimes, he would skip it and just have the oatmeal, I say.

This staggers Prof. M. Mittman who all the sudden can't talk and just flings himself back in his chair before asking me again.

—Oatmeal, he croaks. Are you sure?

—Always with the jam, I say with firmness. No sugar.

And then I lean back and snatch up some paper and also act like I'm making the purposeful note to myself. Meantime the professor is moaning like he's waking from the deep dream.

—Oatmeal, oatmeal. Whole grains, husked groats...who would have thought? Who could have imagined? Never at all would I have suspected, but now of course it makes perfect sense. Absolute perfect sense. In fact, there is probably no more apt description of his narratology. It's his most salient quality.

The professor throws himself back in his chair again and he puts his hands over his long face and beak nose like he's going to have the big breakdown.

—Oatmeal! My god.

—It was always a powerful moment, I say with seriousness.

—And with the jam and coffee and the morning shave... it's extraordinary.

—Don't skip the ablutions, I say.

—The key to everything, the heart of his work, the breakfast. I knew it. But oats, who could have imagined? No wonder he wrote what he did. Such anger, such vision!

We both stay silent, respecting my discovery. Outside the window I see one of the dump boats capsizing all its garbage in the water. The professor is still suffering his attack.

—Now for lunch… I start after awhile.

—No, no! That's enough! cries Prof. M. Mittman and he jumps up like the man with the electrical shock and he waves me down. No more! We have to stop here. Don't say anything further! What you've said is extraordinary enough. It overturns nearly all the conventional thinking on McLemore and I need time to digest it, even if it all aligns with what I've long believed about him. We can analyze his lunch, and perhaps even his afternoon snacks, later. For now, let's concentrate on the significance of this event.

And then the professor stops the tape machine. Even though the air-con is still roaring full-blast, Prof. M. Mittman is breathing hard like he just has run the ten-mile race and his sweating and suffering almost seems to be getting worse. And then unfortunately he stands and holds out his hand and so once more I am forced to take his wet rag fingers.

—I'm completely overwhelmed, he says. These have been monumental revelations, far beyond anything I could have hoped. Your views and observations of McLemore paint a completely different picture of how we understand him and his work. Utterly transformative. I think it's safe to say that in one afternoon you've shed more insight into his writing than all the years of scholarship on him combined.

X.

Despite my good session with Prof. M. Mittman, however, I am still not exited from the woods. For as we are riding home, the professor says that as soon as he can recover himself from our overwhelming discussion he wants to go to Yan Bao to find Mr. McLemore's lost book and for me to show him where. For now he is waiting on the man at the hotel to get him the car since all the taxis and autos in Tandomon are snatched up by the tourists. But when he gets the ride we will go at once, says the professor, and likely by then the TV person can be there to make the report of the big moment.

Now here is the new problem that I scold myself for not considering and so during my long walk home I am pounding my thoughts over what to do. For the other smaller thing that occurs on the ride is that the professor alights me first so I need to quick-think up the smart address for the driver man. From the top of my head, I then give him the number of Cousin Peng's black-and-white on Raiders Hill, a place that when we arrive Prof. M. Mittman looks like he is much approving. It's the quiet night and when I climb out from the car, Cousin Peng's beautiful wife and the *Ah Nia* sisters all come out on the porch to see who's there. I wait until the driver man turns around and roars away, then give my wave to the beautiful sisters and go trudging down the hill.

So following my take forever walk home, the day is already over when I am back in my small flat. But then a strange thing happens: instead of going to my chair to black out from my tiredness or cooking up the big dinner since I am ready to devour the horse, for some reason I go into my bedroom and take out all my old writings from underneath my bedframe.

Ha!, I have not looked at such pieces in many years, though why I want to do so now I am truly not sure. But I haul them out anyway from their big envelopes, blow the dust away, and look again at these pages that start coming back to me with all the people and plots I wrote about long time ago. It's almost like paging through the family union album and for the few moments I am glad to see such again. But soon a dismal feeling begins to creep up on me. For skimming these pages I also recall the giant efforts I put into composing these books that no one knows about and that now do nothing except sleep forgotten under my bed. Maybe Cousin Peng can remember I wrote all these plots but likely not, I think. Even myself lying two feet above every night for twenty years has learned to disregard them. All of which makes me think that if the person had informed me at the start that this is how my writings will end up, I would have spent my life in the different manner.

Besides this though, there is another reason why I neglect looking at these piles of writings for so long. For truth is, whenever I do take the glance I always find myself disrelishing them, particularly after they got rejected by this notable publisher or that A-1 agency. It's as if the volume has gotten cursed from being stamped not worthy so that when I read it later all I see are the mistakes and argly writing and I cannot glimpse anything either that I am approving of. Even now leafing through these old stories, I try not to look at the parts so closely.

Of course adding to my feeling is the gnawing mystery of why these pages got rejected and not the other persons? How many times did I ask myself over the years, Why did this or that edition get printed and praised but not mine? Which significant book person did the choice for that piece of writing over the other? (And also, Why did so many people buy such afterward?) For most of the books that get circulated are not like Mr. Stevenson or Mr. Maugham, but the middle kind of stories, the ones that don't have such great differences in them. So if the reader doesn't like the volume about the lady with the romance from the last century, he can just pick up the plot of the man on the sinking boat or the detective arresting his lover's killer. It's like when the stall runs out of beef noodles so the customer changes his favorite to *bok chor mee* and goes away happy, anyway. But who chooses who makes the dish? Even today as the finisher of six done manuscripts, and the bookstall owner for twenty years next July who has seen all manners of volumes in all different styles, I am stumped by this puzzle.

And besides this, there are the works by the writers like Mr. McLemore that fire up the scholars such as Prof. M. Mittman, but that only seem to me the cannot get through type and leave me further blur over why important persons read such.

So thinking this over, I decide to take out one of my old editions to see after all these years if any light can be shed. The writing I then select is likely the one I relish best. Such is called *Rotten Fruits* and tells the fascinating story of the small Tandomon village that tries to promote itself to get the tourists. So since the area is famous for growing litchis, the officials stage a first-ever litchi festival and invite the reporters from all over the country to come visit to talk to Miss Queen Litchi and enjoy the special delicacies they are preparing, like litchi *ice kachang*, litchi cakes, litchi in coconut milk, litchi drinks and so on. But thing is, the days before the big celebration, the thundering rains come and knock out the electric power and fridges to the village and then right after that the officials have to go pick the wet litchis. So the fruit they gather is quickly rotted but it gets put into the foods anyway since the reporters are flocking to the festival. So the writers eat the litchi foods and suffer the sick diarrhea from the spoiled fruits and then go back home and write up their bad stories. So the village's plan is ruined. Most unfortunate however, is that one of the reporters and Miss Litchi get to fall in love during the festival but after the reporter gets better, he and Miss Litchi discover they cannot be together since her very sight keeps making him go *lao sai* all over again. And so at the finish he puts himself in the water and dies. The end.

This tragedy I think was based on the true story.

Another fascinating book I wrote before that is called *Don't Go Home Again* and now I take out this too, for my long-time inspection. This story is about the beautiful Tandomon singer who goes on to be famous in China and worldwide but also has the bad luck in love and returns home to her country village and meets again her childhood friend who now is the humble man with the small goat and chicken farm and they fall in love and have a happy time but then right at the end he gets the incurable disease and dies.

This I think was also the true story from *The Tandomon Talker*.

For a long time I sit on the floor of my room and scan these pages I spent my years laboring over but they are just like before and still don't tell me how they got disapproved. Maybe writing is like the religion, I think, and not so explainable, otherwise the people would lose their interest and stop practicing. Maybe there's the higher book powers nobody can know about. And so could be these pages are not fully to blame.

But even if I'm not so affronted now (Ha!, so maybe, too that feeling is vanished), I begin to think that these results are not so impressive for all my time bent over the black Royal typewriter that is the same kind Mr. Hemingway used. Just a dusty stack of paper filled up with the different arrangements of words and letters. Not like the big science discovery or the famous cure for the terrible disease or the new building for the widows and orphan children. What good was all of it? No persons got entertained by these pages and nobody like Mr. Yeoh ever read them to his school class for enjoyment. And of course such will never be the case. Maybe I should throw these writings away, I think, and then maybe they can stop plaguing me, like the argly rug that every day you don't notice but still aggrieves the back of your mind. And then suddenly this strikes me as being the exact right thing I should do, so forgetting my growling stomach and drooping eyes I go downstairs to find the sack to throw these works into so I can go to the garbage yard and toss out forever.

But just as I'm piling all my volumes into the plastic bag I get another strange feeling and stop. For it strikes me that if I throw away such writings I could be vexed in the future that they no longer exist since what would happen if one day I decide I need them? Then I would feel worse, I think, especially if someone asks about the years I labored and I would have no proof, even if this just looks like a wasted mash-up of time to me now. And considering this I realize once more that I am of the same character as my customers that also don't like to throw away the books, even if mine are not really books since they never got printed. It is a peculiar thing to feel this way over the rejected stacks of paper with typing on it for these are not like the gold diamonds or family heirlooms to give up. Or even the vacation souvenir. But never mind, this is now my stronger feeling so instead of casting away my pages I wrap them up again in their dusty envelopes and put them into the suitcase to go back to sleep under my bedframe. Probably again for the next twenty years, I think. Although as I'm doing so I then consider that no matter if these writings stay with me or not, I likely will be suffering some kind of vexation, so that in either case the situation is of no one winning. It's much too late now to be anything different.

XI.

Early the next day I go to Tandomon Suffering Martyrs to visit my old school friend Gao who's back in the hospital with the bad case of poisoning from the headglue he used to put on his monkey weave hair. He croaks out the few words about how he has the throbbing pain from his lame leg and also the dizzy feeling in his head, and I tell him how Cousin Peng got ticketed and almost went to jail for attacking the blind tourist with his big knife. Then after we finish exchanging the pleasantries, I ask Gao if I can lend his rumbly Japanese moto-bike for the short while. He doesn't reply anything to this or ask me why I need such but his wife goes into her purse right away for the key and tells me to keep as long as I want. Truth is, I think my friend Gao is relieved at this, too.

Now it's years since I rode the moto-bike but because the tourists have snatched up all the cars across the nation and are grabbing away the taxis, too, there is no other way for the person to go to Yao Ban. So even though I am worrying about riding such a rumbly machine over confusing roads for the distance of two hundred kilometers to the opposite side of Tandomon, and remembering also that I frequently mashed up the moto-bike I did have because I was the small man on top of the big engine, I put the pack of items on my back and head off.

But riding Gao's noisy moto-bike is only the tip of my nervous iceberg. More worrying is what is going to happen when I get to Yan Bao, since could be there's still people there with the facts about Mr. McLemore that can trip me up with the professor. And could be too, that such persons possess the lowdown scoops over how Mr. McLemore operated as the agent man and how he managed his threatening events, such as trickily impersonating that treacherous intelligence man, or hunting down the two-faced traitor at the countryside border, or loving up the beautiful spy at the foreign embassy. Mr. McLemore must have had the army of skills to pull off such deceits, I think, and why Prof. M. Mittman remains not interested in these matters is for me still the peculiar fact.

So while I'm enduring my long boresome ride, considering these turmoils of Mr. McLemore speeds away the time. Otherwise for hours the journey is just the green grasses and high mountains and sometimes the farms with the water buffalo, and then the rattling trucks and bicycles on the road. Not even the train tracks go lying through here, I see. The only thing I do glimpse on this dragging trip are the signs that sprout every few kilometers declaring *Delicious ice kachang!* with an arrow pointing to the house by the roadside. All these are different lettered but they all claim the same thing so after reading such for a long time, I finally decide to jump off the big engine and go up to the house with my mouth watering over the sweet treat. But the *Ah Soh* that replies to the door only gives me the strange look when I ask and says she's not the *ice kachang* seller and closes fast. So then I get back on the moto-bike and go until the next sign but get the exact answer again. Finally after I do this twice more, I press the *Ah Soh* to come to the roadside and I point to the sign. After reading it, she makes the surprised face like I'm the Mars man and says she's never noticed such announcements before and hastes back into the house. Tandomon persons can sometimes vex the patience, I tell you.

At last though, just when the road has become dirt and is almost turned to grass I see the torn-up board in English and Chinese spelling out *Kong Xie Plantations*, even though I probably would have rumbled past if I wasn't being the careful watcher. For even to me riding hours through the green grasses and high mountains, this place looks like the middle of nowhere, with no wood buildings or smoking trucks or any persons cutting up the fields. And it strikes me as regrettable that the notable person like Mr. McLemore has to come here to die, though it double-confirms the saying that everyone starts out helpless in the life and concludes himself the same way.

Also I don't think the area is the tobacco plantation like the newspaper death stories say, since instead of the small leafy plants on the grounds, all I see are the rows of the dragon fruit trees to the edge of a big river. (Ha, so I was correct over this detail!) Viewing such, I wonder how the smart reporter man thinks the tobacco plant can be the fruit tree but then I remember that the newspaperman's job is to make the story, not always tell the truth.

So first thing, I start scouring for the suitable place to put the tribute to Mr. McLemore. Because all the spiny rows look nothing special I climb off the moto-bike and trudge to the river that has the wide brown water that smells like the mix of rotted fruits and the shrimp factory. When I get to the front row of dragon trees, I then count off eight trees for good luck, haul out my small shovel and start digging at the ground in front. Fortunate for me, the earth is wet so I don't strain my aching muscles and I don't dig across any tree roots, either. Then after the hole is big enough I take out the large-size Milo jar that has all the writings I created, wrap such in the plastic bag and drop it down, before filling the ground back up with old dirt and pacing off to the river. Of course this is not the most outstanding tribute spot but it views directly onto the water and also will not be so burdensome to find later. Overall I'm thinking that after the long trip, Prof. M. Mittman likely won't be so questioning when we get to searching and finally stumble onto these pages. I then find another short tree that's not the dragon fruit and relieve myself.

After this though, I don't go back to the moto-bike. Instead I look across the brown river that is the border for the Tandomon nation and I reconsider more about Mr. McLemore ending up here. Now I'm thinking he chose this spot on purpose because of his adventuresome business. Could be that he needed to stay here to make the risky dashes into the other nation, or maybe he got kicked out of that country but had to remain close by to conduct such affairs as contacting his networks of foreigners or eating the dinners with the double spy. Such are the regular routines for the danger agent, I have learned from my danger books, along with having the big estate and fancy house, even if from where I stand I cannot see such lodgings. From what I informed him, Prof. M. Mittman likely is expecting the old-style English bungalow and if there is none I might have to say it got torn down since.

But since I am deep into my thoughts, I am not noticing that beside me now is a bent old auntie with a face like a wrinkled thunderstorm and pointing at me the big shovel that is stinking of cow manure.

—What you want here? she says in a voice like she wants to pound me on the head with the long tool. And before I can reply back she raises it up and asks again.

Now fortunate for me, my small shovel is in my pack so I am not looking like the person out here to cause the disturbance. And so smoothly in the calm voice and the serious expression

I just say that I was out walking and so had the snack by the river, although as I'm replying this I can also see the auntie is not believing any of this smoke. Why does anyone want to eat the lunch foods here before the smelling water? I can hear her thinking, and so maybe I really am the thief or the running away man doing no good. But because at the moment I happened to be pondering about Mr. McLemore, I then bring up his name to show that I'm not the total stranger and ask, Is this plantation where the notable writer Lawrence McLemore once lived?

Instead of relaxing though, the *Ah Mm* just grips the shovel tighter before allowing that such is the place and giving me more of the thunderstorm face.

—What you want about him? she asks, and because now I am growing somewhat concerned, I say that I admire Mr. McLemore's writings and I'm investigating his life.

But the auntie doesn't seem to like this answer better than the others and now I'm almost readying myself for the painful blow when she lowers down the tool.

—So you take the box then, she says, giving me the manure shovel. And then suddenly like she's speaking to the captured person she orders me to follow her, though when I ask her where we're going, she barks "Save talk!" and I don't question anymore.

So now we are trudging along the river under the hot sun with the smells from the mud banks coming up and all the mosquitoes freely taking their bites. Until finally after the long march we come around to a big cement building. This is not the English bungalow like I mentioned to Prof. M. Mittman but more resembling the place where the secondary or college students stay, though it might be the prison, too. But then as we come closer, I see that poking up from behind is the small building painted gold and white like the temple and I start to smell the incense, too. And now I am glad I have on the covered shirt and long pants for I did not know that today I would be coming to the religious place.

So at the door I lay down the shovel and we go under the wooden sign saying *New True Way Buddhist Temple* and into the cement room. Now it's dark here and my eyes are blind for the moment but when I recover I see a group of boy monks in their gray robes crammed together on the big couch looking at me. They got the game show on at the loud volume, but then the auntie snaps them something in Chinese and right away two of them go outside and the other cuts off the TV like they've been doing the bad thing. The auntie also glares at them with her thunderstorm face and now I don't feel so chastised.

After a couple of minutes, the two boy monks come back lugging the big box like a steamer trunk that's covered in the thick-inch dust.

—All his things, the auntie says. Long time here so you take away now.

And then she gives me the ordering look again. But this is so surprising that I cannot believe.

—These belong to Mr. McLemore? I ask with wonder. The *Ang Moh* Englishman?

My expression is now hanging open in the A to Z surprise.

—Okay, you take away now, says the auntie. Fifty dollar to keep. Long time here.

No words come to my tongue so the auntie snaps up again.

—Storage cost, please. *Boh lui* cannot have!

Fortunate for me I have the amount and pay it over. But still I am not knowing what to say. Can these truly be Mr. McLemore's final possessions? Why has no one since claimed these important chattels?

—Have car? the auntie asks after she counts away my money and I shake my head.

—Moto-bike, I reply.

—Moto-bike! How you get home then? exclaims the auntie. Why you want this?

Now she's the one who's looking surprising at me.

—Mr. McLemore was the notable person, I manage to say. His things are the significant possessions.

As soon as I say this a couple of the boy monks give out the barking laugh before the auntie scowls them down. But I don't hear this so much because I'm eyeballing the trunk to see if I can break such open and glimpse the insides so maybe I don't have to lug everything back. But the lock is big and rusty like the mummy tomb, and it will be no way, I conclude. When I look back at the auntie, I see she's got the laughing face on now, too. So this is my chance to acquire some facts, I decide.

—Is this everything he got? How long did Mr. McLemore stay here?

The auntie crinkles up her storm face.

—One year, maybe longer, she says. Long time ago.

—He live inside here? Where did he stay?

The auntie crooks her head to the window.

—He stay in the shed by the machines, *lah!*, and a boy monk snickers again. He black out on the floor. Have no bed. Not so many things, either!

The auntie's words deliver me a powerful shock. In the shed? Sleeping on the floor? Now I am wondering if we are conversing over the same Mr. McLemore, though of course I know it cannot be otherwise. But why does he do this? Such is not the manner of the important danger man or the notable writer. Is she saying that Mr. McLemore was living like the person without the possessions?

—Why he stay out there? I ask.

The auntie slashes her finger over her throat.

—No money, *lah*! No money!

Mr. McLemore a poor person? I take another moment to digest this next hard fact. Why should the *Who's Who* man with the long catalog of books be treated like the dog living in the wooden box in a far-off plantation? Such is making no sense at all. It is like no one is here knowing who he really is. Then also why didn't he speak up and announce himself?

And then in the flash it strikes me like bricks that this must have been part of the bigger operation; that Mr. McLemore got ordered to lay low like this on the crucial super-secret mission. This is the only reason I can conjure to explain him being in the situation to impersonate the man with no funds. Truly it must have been the most powerful assignment, I am now thinking, and truly his life must have been in the most immediate danger. As I'm looking out the window to the place where he dwelled his last days, it's coming clear to me that even I was severely underestimating Mr. McLemore's talents and what he got commanded to do.

—Did any of the visitors come to see him? I ask. Like the foreign people?

—Only police, says the auntie. But he always run off to hide. He says they want to arrest him for taking big money in Thailand. But maybe not so big if he lives here!

And now I am getting the full-truth picture. With all the powerful officials breathing his tracks, no wonder Mr. McLemore was hiding here. He must have been trapped like the caged animal looking for the way out. I wonder which government he was assigned for and if he could even be the double spy. Such is the most jeopardous situation of all, I know from my plentiful readings.

—What did Mr. McLemore do when he was here? I ask. How did he have the money?

—He pick the field, says the auntie, but only when he not drinking so much. He like the English gin if he can afford. If not, the Chinese wine, *lah!*

And now the group of boy monks start giggling up again. But I am not hearing such at all. Instead I am marveling at the sacrifices Mr. McLemore made, and how just like the undercover man in the agent books no one can ever understand his true picture or what he goes through. Except now for me since I am the one piecing it together. So maybe I am becoming the small kind of danger man, too. But there's still some more difficult facts I need to know and so not dwelling over my distress I ask the auntie the next hard question.

—How did Mr. McLemore die?

Soon as I pose this, though, the boy monks get silent and even the auntie is quiet. This must be the worst detail of all and I feel myself getting a dreadness over what she is about to say. But then the auntie gives a loud shout and the adult monk wearing the gray robe and dark glasses quickly comes in. After she makes the command in Chinese, all the boy monks raise off the couch with sour faces and he takes them away. The auntie then waits until the room gets empty before she talks again.

—His fault, she says in the whisper. He die one night in the river. He steal the boat and try to cross over but the boat went down. He can't swim so the water swallowed him up. I think the crocodile must have some bites, too.

Hearing this, my heart freezes up, glimpsing in my mind the terrible fleeing, the thrashing in the water, maybe the gunshots blazing. And then the hero death by oneself at night.

—Why is he going across? I ask, trembling a little.

The auntie doesn't reply right away. It's like she is deeply thinking over the human event that's almost too much to bear. It is the powerful moment that passes.

—He want to go to the Malay side, she finally says. He think about it full-time and ask me, too. He says he want to go to the fuckshop there. But I tell him there's no place like that over there. No Malay girls working by the river! I say. You have to go to the other island side! But he don't listen and sneak out that night and steal the boat. He said he make it before. But he don't listen and got swallowed! Crocodile eat, too! Now wait, wait the minute. You no move.

The auntie bustles out before coming back with an old burlap sack and a heavy expression like she's been brooding over the sorrowful things. Or maybe she just needs to do the last purposeful act she forgot about. I see she's now got on the thick gloves, too. Without saying which she's thinking, she hands the sack to me.

—His ash, she says. You take away too, okay?

XII.

Next morning I am sleeping at Gecko 88 past the opening time and it is not until Charlie O. is banging at the door for the long time that I finally rouse myself. Now it is not my custom to black out all night at my stall but after coming back late from Yao Ban with the chest of Mr. McLemore's important possessions, I had the flood of tiredness and could not even go home to my small rooms. Before I left that place, the boy monks lashed the heavy trunk to my person with the long ropes and so sitting straight up I drove the rumbly moto-bike all the way back to Tandomon City. Around my neck too, was hanging the burlap sack of Mr. McLemore's ash so I cannot move anything other than my hands and feet for the long hours. When I finally arrived at my door of Gecko 88, I tumbled off the moto-bike before dragging inside the chest and falling into my chair for the night.

However Charlie O. has woken me this morning with the good news. He and his friend have all made up, he announces, and he's leaving again for Thailand. Everything was just the misunderstanding, and he is here to say thank you for hearing my problems and please come one day to the Thailand house they will be living at. He then takes my hand and says he'll miss me and that I'm the true friend he's got. All the others either desert him or shy away. So like in all good events there is also the painful side, I think, and as we have our chat I consider how long I know Charlie O. and about his new turn and how the life cannot ever said to be finished. Although like I said, most often these turning affairs happen to the others, not myself.

But then after Charlie O. finishes his tea, I have to open my stall. And already as I'm swinging the gate, the customers are pouring in like rain, wanting this detective book or that romance story or trying to peddle that box of paper editions they don't like to read. (Ha!, for I always think that if you don't want such, why you believe others not feel the same?) And so for the next hours even though I am still dropped dead from my weariness, I am fetching down books or arguing over the sales even if all I am wanting is to crack open Mr. McLemore's last things, especially now since I realize how I undervalued his talents and how he got heroically deceased trying to make the contact with the dangerous prostitute spy. It's like the real-life mystery that's buried inside the trunkcase by my front door and all morning long I think about how Mr. McLemore was lying low from the agents in the machine shed and got swallowed up by the river at the nation border. But it's not until the afternoon comes and the customers go away that I at last have the chance to drag the heavy box by my register and attack the rusty lock.

For such the big latch it falls off with just two strikes from my iron bar. But just before I open the contents I stop. For while I am not so much the superstitious person, since I think that worrying over where to step your foot or when to cross the fingers brings the bad luck by itself, lifting the lid off Mr. McLemore's trunk gives me the uneasy feeling. Already I'm wondering if maybe I will find the dangerous photographs or the secret documents I shouldn't glimpse. Perhaps these discoveries can even give me treachery and force me to hide my tracks. So very carefully I open off the cover.

First thing that hits me though is the smell of old things. This cloud is so powderful I got to lift up the case wide and walk away so it can dissolve itself. Even then I need to put the fan at high volume so it doesn't leave the *pong* inside my stall and drive away the purposeful customers. When I come back, I furthermore spray the Lysol can all around before I start digging in.

Second thing I see is that there's nothing of Mr. McLemore's personal items inside except for the few clothes arising all the bad smells. There's no billfold wallet or rusty handgun or even the family pictures, and I'm surprised until I consider that this is the kind of impersonal condition that must be the usual situation for all the danger men. And so my respect climbs even more despite my holding my nose away and being overall disappointed.

Of course because Mr. McLemore is still the notable writer, I do see that underneath the bad-odor clothes is the shelf of thick volumes on the trunk bottom. (Ha, so he also is the person who cannot throw away the books!) The first copies are all his own writings, but beside them is the row of even dustier volumes of the kind I have never seen before and that are lined-up according to the alphabet. Here must be the valuable possessions of the notable writer, I think, and now I am ready to dive in fully to examine them to get the truthful insight to the workings of his creative mind.

But unfortunately just as I am going to begin my study, a complaining mother suddenly rushes in with her crying boy to *kau peh* over the crams books I sold her the month ago, saying that such are out-of-date and have all the wrong answers. As the result she now is accusing, her boy has to go repeat the form and cannot enter the junior college. I ought to get the ticket for the deceiving advertising, she goes on, since her son used to be the most promiseful student before he mugged my books. Now he's dropped to the bottom rank. Of course this is never mind that I also have seen this crying boy several times before on Bao Lao Street just playing time wasting time; instead his ireful mother is wailing that because he cannot attend the junior institute, his future path has been corrupted since now he won't get into the regular college, and following that he won't get the admittance to the London School of Economics and it is all for me to blame.

London School, ha! The only way this crying boy can make it to such a place is if they got the snooker table in the classroom. But I don't say anything to this complaining mother because unlike Angry Lim, the customer is always corright to me and I also am too weary to bark back, and so now I just soothe her and for free give her the different text that I say can correct her crying boy's path. Never mind that the volume I hand her is the home economics book; I say it has much to do with the London School and by the time this boy can figure out the difference, the lessons about cleaning the home and eating the nutritious foods are likely better for him, anyway. So in the end she thanks me and the boy stops his crying and they go off but still I have wasted the precious half-hour that I could be investigating Mr. McLemore's last things.

So finally I can return to the trunkcase and I pull out the old books again. And just to make sure I cannot be bothered, I off the lights and close the door to keep away the demanding customers. But it's then that I make my first terrible discovery. For since I am in the book business twenty years next July, I cannot help myself but get intrigued by the strange volumes at the bottom of Mr. McLemore's case, never mind that they just look like more dusty editions. It's like the man whose career is to study bugs and that goes on the foreign vacation but everywhere he travels he's always looking in the dirt, anyway. So I pile these books on my desk and start to examine.

The first thing I can see is that these bindings are much aged, maybe a hundred years old and more, and a few got the cello tape all over their torn covers. Others got the moldy stains and peeling backs, and one volume looks like it was scorched up in the fire, too. Now because these are so out-of-date I never heard of any of these titles so I start to browse with curiosity and after a few minutes I begin reading the one with the fiery cover called *The Tribulations of Lord Hogg on His Time in Cape Colony* since it seems like the adventure kind of story.

However this is not the easy chore and soon I find myself getting beat down by this writer's words. Even though the lively action is going on, just like in Mr. McLemore's books this one also has the butterfly sentences that go on and on to nowhere and the mash-up story that's mainly the cock show. In this plot, the man Lord Hogg has got the short circuit in the head, and he speaks and acts peculiar and all his friends behave the same like they just come out of the dream. At the same time, everyone is plotting against him for the money while also scheming for the beautiful girl that is mixed up between good and evil but is too *mong cha cha* to decide and because of this then has the breakdown, and dot dot dot and so on since overall the writer of this dusty book isn't greatly bothered to explain how such is taking place. Hard enough to read such a tangle when I am in the alert mood but now this is truly digging the hard ditch.

However, after a few dozen pages of drudging I start to get a funny feeling like the Hogg man in the book. Not only are the sentences sounding like those I read before, but some of the characters also are like I know them from before. And so I search my mind…where? And then it strikes me: this is the similar story to Mr. McLemore's notable novel, *Footprint in the Water*. In fact the mash-up plot is exactly the same with the forgetting man and the cheating friend and the killer that dies from the blade. And then there is the same *Ah Nia* who switches her mind and bawls over the Lord Hogg who went off and disappeared on her. This is the strangest occurrence, I think to myself and because I am wondering that there's surely some mistake, I quickly take the copy of Mr. McLemore's book and browse through to the correct spot and begin to check carefully. And after several minutes of comparing, I find that I am confirmed.

In all my twenty years in the bookstall business next July, I never once encountered this kind of example, though occasionally *Serious Books Digest* or *The South-East Asiatic Literary Review* does the story of this notable writer attacking that notable writer for robbing away some of his plot, even if the books they discuss about don't seem so worthy to steal in the first place, and in the end nobody admits they *kapo* anything one way or the other. But because now I am fully confused, I go back to check the printing date of this fiery book. And it's then I experience my unfortunate event. For right on the front page under the writer's name of Mr. Alastair Faltermore, the Hogg volume firmly states it was circulated in 1831. And not only that but also stamped in the wax seal in the corner is the sentence: *Property of Penang Free School.*

I cannot sufficiently tell you the horrigible feeling that rises up in me. It's like what happens when one eats the *prawn mee* in the morning that was left overnight by the shady hawker and then hours later gets the sharp pains in the stomach. And I'm starting to feel my pounding headache coming on, too. So in the haste I fetch down my careful notes from the Tandomon National

Library est. 1914 and open up the copy of *The Crying Bandicoot*, which is the plot about the beat-up jockey that blackmails the sweet *Ah Nia* who loves the doctor's son that needs to escape to the USA and so on. I then root around the other volumes laying on my desk and begin browsing these. And soon I find the one with the peeling back called *Adventures at Epsom Fair* that is printed in 1816 and in front is stamped *Albion Secondary School Library*, and that when I go match it side-by-side with Mr. McLemore is again the same for all the writing I check.

And even still I cannot believe. For more proof I go study the book by Mr. McLemore called *My Stolen Life*. But this plot I see comes from the 1847 volume named *The Hedges of Twickenham* that was lended by the Penang Free School and hardly looks scanned. In fact I notice this one has the pages and pages of underlines that fully copy along with Mr. McLemore's sentences since he didn't bother to change such at all.

How can this be?, I now am raging. Suddenly the room is spinning around me and it's like the earth has gone all dark, too. With the deep ireful anger, I now see that Mr. McLemore is not the notable writer worthy of respect. He's just the famous figure pulling wool over the peoples' faces! In truth, he is nothing but the copier of the dusty volumes who has never created the single sentence for his own, even though he circulates all his piles of famous books. His editions do not deserve to sit on the high shelf in their shiny leather bindings to be admired at like all the newspaper death stories and the *Who's Who* say. Mr. McLemore is just the big writer fraud doing smoking mirrors.

But as bitter as this notion is, I then realize my next terrible conclusion. For as I am sitting alone in Gecko 88 lashing myself with my stormful thoughts of Mr. McLemore possessing the esteem that is not his, I start considering the facts about his undercover life and the details the auntie informed me, like where he was living, how he was the drinking man, how he got drowned, and so forth. And the more I chew such, the more I have to conclude that Mr. McLemore also is not the danger man that all the noisy whisperers say he was, or that the reporter stories print up.

How can this cock-up person perform all the urgent duties demanded from such a job? I ask myself. How could he fight away the spies and go gather the secret intelligence from all the governments if he is the fraud and drinking man? Who would hire this kind of person for such affairs? And how come he has not even the one vital paper in his possession when he dies? There are no positive answers that I can conjure to such crucial questions and such notions now seem to me as just the bluffing smoke created by the believe-anything sheep talkers, and then written up by the don't-care-to-check newspaper reporters. There should be some kind of jail penalty for spreading such fraud, I think, especially since it concerns the actions of the true espionage men.

So now even though it is still daylight I shut up my bookstall and sit alone with the big empty feeling. I browse through Mr. McLemore's books some more and discover other certain facts, like how he can take the two or three parts from one book and mix it with some of the others so not everything looks the same, or how he can use the different character names but then keep everything else like it was. Searching in his stenchful trousers, I then find a big bill for the liquors he drank, as well as the long-ago ticket from the Thailand officials telling him when to arrive at the court on such and such a date to face the charge of stealing the money. This completes the picture, I conclude, and it has been the long long time since I have felt so low for myself.

So I am just storing away this heavy trunkcase and not wanting to ever address these contents anymore or think about what this means with my trying to be the notable writer, when the telephone rings and the official man right away is demanding to know if I am Mr. Cecil Po. Yes, I'm here, I say, and after this there is some noise on the wire before the man replies good, because he's calling from the American Embassy in Tandomon and would like me to come down at once on the important business. For a moment I can't hear nothing for the hot blood ringing in my ears and when my voice cries out, Why? I only get more wire noises. But then the man comes back to say not to worry since such has nothing to do with me but only that they want to ask me a few questions to clear up some matters. Reason is that Prof. M. Mittman is currently being seized there and for the long time he's been requesting my name.

XIII.

I never before have been involved with the USA government so first thing I do is run home on the moto-bike and change to my special white suit with the extra double pleats that fortunately I have not yet packed away in the moth flakes. Then I race over to Lam Hoon Street for Arun the barber to give me the quick shave-up and haircut, and I am in and out in five minutes. When this is done I buzz over to the tall colonial building on top of Raiders Hill that's higher even than Cousin Peng's house, show my picture to the guards and can be brought inside.

In the ice-cold room there, Prof. M. Mittman is waiting for me with the much distressed look, along with an *Ang Moh* American lady with cat glasses and bird nest hair busy at shuffling the stack of urgent reports. Such a place looks exactly like the tax room I have to go to sometimes when the collection person sends me the demanding note to ask over this and that profits I have earned, and so I begin sweating as I come in. But no one barks at me as I enter now and instead the professor's face turns to gladness and the bird nest lady lays down her crucial papers and invites me to take the chair.

—Thank you for coming, she says, and I say it is not the problem for me and also no, I don't want the water to drink, but I do have the seat. I then make the nod to the professor and give him the reassuring smile and am about to ask him directly over his difficulty when the inviting lady changes back to her distressed expression and starts orating like the action barrister.

—Mr. Mittman was arrested today on a fairly significant offense, she says. Fortunately, it looks like everything has been cleared up but there are a few things we need to know. And he's been asking for you ever since he was taken into custody.

Arrested?! What kind of mischief can the university scholar create? Prof. M. Mittman is not the thieving man or the waving-the-knife around type like Cousin Peng. And of course he's not the pirate kind. Maybe it was the drinking or an affray with the stranger, I consider. Cannot be the sexual matters, I don't think.

—What kind of offenses? I say with my heart pounding hard.

The cat glasses lady shuffles her papers for the correct urgent report.

—The first charge was the attempted theft of precious remains, she says. There was also a lesser offense of outraging the modesty of a minor. But as I said, both charges were dropped. It was all a mistake. There are no criminal matters now pending against Mr. Mittman.

Now never before have I known of such crimes, but hearing such makes me think that Prof. M. Mittman maybe is the peculiar man and so I again glimpse his face, which now looks truly abashed but doesn't give the hint. I think I am completely lost over what is occurring.

—How did he get arrested? I say.

It's a complicated story, says the bird nest lady who now looks like she doesn't want to mention such regrettable details unless she's forced. But then she goes ahead and does it, anyway.

According to her, the matter came up when the professor made the arrangements with Big Yoshi to rent the car to go to

Yan Bao. However, since all the other cars have been snatched by the tourists Big Yoshi had to give him the black hearse automobile that he uses in his charnel business. Only thing is that he failed to tell his Malay wife who already had rented such for the Chan family funeral and who were gathered around when Prof. M. Mittman jumped in and drove off with the dead person body of *Ah Pek* Chan.

Because the professor was angry when he got stopped and cursed at the family, the officials also seized him for offending the feeling of the girl child Mei Chan, she adds.

All through her explaining, Prof. M. Mittman sits like the big meek man. When the cat glasses lady is done, he looks up and puts his hands in the air like he's giving up.

—I'm truly sorry, he says. But just as she said, it was all a misunderstanding. I had no idea there was a body in the car. That man Yoshi didn't say anything.

—That's right, says Missus Cat Glasses. Mr. Yoshimoto confirms it was all a complete accident. He's apologized to the family and they're willing to forget the entire incident. And Mr. Mittman has apologized, as well. So that's been resolved.

Now I am in the state of knowing but still being confused. If the problem is forgotten already why does the professor have to stay in this cold room to chin wag the official lady, and then call me up to make me talk to the USA government? In fact why are they harassing the man in this position in the first place? Did Prof. M. Mittman write something upsetting to the people, or maybe is he the government enemy?

I politely ask the lady again.

—The police want some assurance from us that Mr. Mittman won't be causing any more difficulty while he's here before fully dropping the charges, she says. Mr. Mittman has told us about you and your company and your personal invitation to visit Tandomon. Given your position, we'd be happy to accept your assuming responsibility for him during his visit so we can forget the matter. Is that acceptable to you?

Now I am truly vexed up since every explanation I get only gives me the further snarl. Why is this matter up to me, even if I am the Executive President of the New Pathways Development and Trading Company, the details over which I am trying to forget from my mind as we are talking. Do they think the university scholar will go cause more mischief with the dead bodies? Now Missus Cat Glasses does the sigh and gives me the heavy look, like she's got to inform me some more bad facts.

—According to his visa, Mr. Mittman is currently unemployed and has been so for the last several months. He also has only thirty-one dollars in his possession and no available credit. Technically, he is an undesirable visitor and open to deportation. We want to ensure that he has the means not to become a burden so long as he stays in Tandomon. If you can take responsibility for him, we can release him.

—But he's the college professor! I exclaim. That's his work job! How is he unemployed?

Now this is just as big the shock to me as the professor being arrested. Unemployed means that he's the on-the-street and begging man. Or that he doesn't even have the menial labor. No way can this be true. Maybe I cannot comprehend everything Prof. M. Mittman says, but he still spouts the powerful sentences over the pointless things like all the other college scholars. The lady digs around for more vital documents.

—Mr. Mittman was a teaching assistant at Saylorsville Junior College in Michigan for one semester last year, she reads off the paper. He was fired in June and has not returned. Before that, Mr.

Mittman taught for one summer at the Millard Fillmore Institute of Continuing Education, and was also a junior obedience instructor at the Old Dog/New Tricks Canine School in Saginaw, Michigan.

—I was not fired, interrupts Prof. M. Mittman with the huff in his voice. The semester ended and my appointment was concluded. I am technically now on sabbatical. However I am fully expecting a call regarding my reassignment and I have offers pending from a variety of institutions.

This news now makes me dizzy, like I'm all the way out to sea. I reach into the pocket of my white suit pants with the extra double pleats and find the napkin that was left there twenty years before and wipe my face. The lady goes on.

—Mr. Mittman's last employment was at Wizard's Magic Pizza and Drive-Thru in Saylorsville, she says. He was the weekend grill man and Sorcerer of Sauce on the night shift.

—That was only a temporary circumstance while I was completing my research, says the professor. My discipline is highly specialized and not so easily placeable within the academic spectrum.

The bird nest lady gives Prof. M. Mittman the talk cock look when he says this.

—But what about the big book you're working at? I can barely ask him. And the printer making the extra copies and giving you the more money?

—Why yes, the work is going extremely well thanks largely to your contributions, says the professor who suddenly switches to his horn voice. I should have my first draft finished imminently. It's already exceeding my expectations. As for M. Mittman Scholastic Publications, it is now undergoing a reorganization that will soon result in the significant expansion of staff and resources. I have great hopes for its success.

—But what about the TV story and the camera person making the news report? And the Ford money that's buying the trip?

—I've brought with me all the necessary equipment for the proper documentation of my research, says Prof. M. Mittman continuing on. I'm certain that when completed, the extraordinary account about the rediscovery of a forgotten literary talent will garner great interest from the worldwide media. As for the Ford money, that was my mother's Falcon. She drove it but once a week to electrolysis.

Even though I'm feeling more and more boiled up, I hold onto my thoughts and so does Missus Cat lady. But then she raises up and says she has to leave for the minute and can I make the decision over Prof. M. Mittman? She also asks can I bring the coffee and though mostly I don't like such black mouthwash from the USA, now I say sure, to take my bad taste away.

When we're alone the professor moves his chair near me and puts his dishrag hand on my shoulder.

—I realize this is highly embarrassing, he says, and I apologize for involving you. I can also assure you I never had any intention of stealing Mr. Chan. But let me say also that I think Lawrence McLemore is an undiscovered giant of 20th century literature and that I am on the verge of completing the definitive study of him and his work. Nothing like this currently exists. My book will give him the prominence he deserves. It's the once-in-a-lifetime opportunity.

—Who's going to circulate such a book? I fire back. No book printer wants the writings from a saucemaker doggy trainer. Book circulating the cutthroat business, *lah!* And no one wants to buy the product from the Mittmans Publishers, either.

—There's no one of his stature left, says the professor like he's not heard the word from me. All the great writers have been analyzed a thousand times over. You can stock ten libraries with what's been done on Joyce, on Woolf, on Faulkner. But not McLemore. Not yet. My book, along with his unpublished writing, will put him in the first rank of modern English authors. Such a priceless stroke that it should even exist! We must get to Yan Bao and find it.

And now I find myself filled with the big bitterness and not wanting to further myself any longer with Prof. M. Mittman.

—How are you going to write this famous book? The USA official persons want to deport you back. How can you finish this thing? In the prison house?

—Don't be concerned about appearances, the professor goes on like he's soothing the playground child. Everything can be worked out. The book is what's important and I'm almost done. The only thing missing is McLemore's work. That's what we need to focus on. Think of what this means to literature, what it means to readers of great fiction. And we'll be the ones credited with his rediscovery. Think of having your name, Cecil Po, in the minds of millions of people worldwide and in the notebooks of literature students everywhere.

—This is one big cock-up, I mutter. Not worth the time anymore.

—Just one trip to Yan Bao, just one afternoon of your life and I'll take care of the rest, he says. You owe it to all those wanting readers and all those worthy students. Think of them. And think of the memory of Mr. McLemore himself, a powerful vision neglected and forgotten in his lifetime through no fault of his own. He deserves his own place in the literary canon. As a writer of the utmost significance, he and his reputation need all the help we can give.

—I'm not so sure about that, I say.

XIV.

The next time I see Prof. M. Mittman it is the few days later and we are journeying to Yan Bao and he no longer is wearing the shiny gold watch on his arm, but he does say he has the money now to live in Tandomon. So at least this is one pounding head-ache I am able to avoid.

Unfortunately though, because of his latest troubles Prof. M. Mittman also is being prevented by the officials from renting any-more Big Yoshi's black hearse automobile. And likewise the flood of Tandomon visitors still are snatching up all the other cars for their purposeful tours. So that morning (Ha!, not the afternoon like the professor says), I take out Gao's rumbly moto-bike to make the long trip again. But not exactly like before since now I have along the professor who is the *fatty bom bom* man who leaves scarce room for me on the small small seat, and who also makes the moto-bike jump up in the front when he squats down on the back. So eventually I make the sack of heavy bricks and lash such to the steering handles so the moto-bike stays on the ground, and even though now I am nearly sitting atop the front tire, Prof. M. Mittman grabs his sweaty arms around me to hang tight and we go off.

But this time the journey seems double never-ending and the bigger part of me now is wishing the USA government can reconsider the mistake they made and stop us along the way to ship Prof. M. Mittman back home. For the one thing, with the professor hunching behind, the rumbly moto-bike can only gasp to half the speed and even the smallest road holes give us nearly the constant accidents. Sometimes on the hill even the old man on the bicycle whizzes us by, and every ten yards I'm convinced over our coming breakdown.

Second thing is that the professor has to continually jump off the moto-bike to go relieve himself by the roadside bushes. Every five minutes it seems, he talks in my ear to make the stop and it's like he is drinking the gallon jug in back while I am driving the motor in front. Every time too, the professor gets off he has to dig around his cheap sack for some yellow pills to take, although one time as he's digging he removes by accident the pair of red panties that come from Charlie O.'s friend's office. And so it is my turn to be the American and put away my words while he stuffs such back inside with haste, although when he squats himself again on the moto-bike and rewraps his arms across my waist I now am feeling much less comfortable.

But finally at last, the torn-up sign for the Kong Xie plantation comes up on the rutty road. Now when the professor jumps from the bike he doesn't take out his medicines or the panties but instead has the small movie camera in his big hand. He's going to make the record of us walking to where Mr. McLemore's book is buried, he says, and also take the picture of the important moment when we find such. So telling me to go slow and holding out a stick with a microphone tied on, he follows me along to the river, which is where I stop and say I got to pace off from where I remembered.

—But isn't there a marker somewhere? asks the professor looking around. How do we know where it's buried?

—Just the memory, I say. The servants want to keep it like that. It's the privacy concern for Mr. McLemore.

—Well, are any of them still here? he says, still scanning about. Can we ask any of them?

—All gone. Mr. McLemore's house is torn down and all the butlers scattered and now it's just the Buddhist school.

—Do the Buddhists know?

—They might but they don't say. They all take the silent vows. But don't vex, my mind still recalls this like just the few days ago. Wind up the camera now.

So while the professor rolls his camera on me, I act like I'm going into the difficult trance, trying to piece together the exact steps to where Mr. McLemore's lost writing is covered up. I put the big grimace on my face and look fiercely all around and even go up and touch the leafs of the trees like a healer man, until at last I start walking very inchedly to dragon fruit tree number eight. Then in the truthful gesture I pace off the number of steps from the river and point to a place in the ground and announce that such is the spot.

—This is where we need to do the digging, I say.

Such a declaration makes the professor powerfully excited and he lays down the movie camera and microphone stick and stares at the dirt like it's turning to gold.

—This is an extraordinary moment, he says. Unpublished work from the author of *The Crying Bandicoot*, *The Barber Has Lumbago*, *A Sandwich for Monty*... I can hardly speak. It's literally like the buried treasure.

Prof. M. Mittman looks up at me and it's like the tears might come pouring down his sweaty bread face any second.

—Do you know that even today scholars are debating *Potatoes in the Attic*? Whether it's a novel about a young woman surviving the French Revolution or a man teaching English to natives in the Cameron Highlands? Even today! And still no agreement! It's that complexity, that ambiguity, that makes McLemore such an indescribable writer.

About this I am not feeling so sure. How Mr. McLemore can be the powerful writer if people are not knowing what he means is something I cannot figure, even if I have likewise read this opinion in the newspaper death stories. So I ask the professor.

—Which is it? I say. What theme do you think Mr. McLemore was trying to express?

Prof. M. Mittman twitches his beak nose and gives himself the big pause, like he's thinking over the final exam problem.

—That's such a difficult question, he finally says. Really, I don't know if I can even begin to answer that. But let me say this. Even though I've naturally never read the book, only its summary, I believe that *Potatoes in the Attic* is McLemore's vision of what the Malay natives *might* have thought about the French Revolution *if* they'd only heard of it. And of course, in the words "might" and "if," therein lies the tragedy.

And then the professor looks at the dirt with more sorrowfulness.

—Let's dig the ground, I say.

Now for this the professor steps away to arrow me, saying he wants to capture the important moment when the lost writings are discovered. So aiming the camera he does the eye power while I sweat and grunt and tear up the dirt with my small shovel. But the curious thing is that even after digging the hole big around as the rice barrel and deep like a washtub I am still not finding the Milo jar, and with every empty scoop Prof. M. Mittman is becoming more and more anxious. Finally while he goes off to relieve himself in the river I take a stand back to relook the situation. For now I am wondering if maybe a watcher person followed me that day and stole away the writing.

It's then that I see the front row of trees is not so even like before and so I go and inspect closer. And that's when I find that where the number one tree used to be, there is now only the stump like someone has lately come and chopped such to bits. So while the professor grumbles about all the film that's being wasted even though he's still only giving the eye power, I recount the dragon trees and start uprooting in front of number seven. And very directly I discover the old Milo jar and Prof. M. Mittman is shaking with excitement.

I hand the jar to him and for the few moments his talking stops and he can only look at the pages inside.

—So here it is, he finally says. It actually exists. I just knew he had unpublished work. This is the literary find of a lifetime.

And then he slowly twists open the writing.

First thing he says, though, after he removes such is to express his puzzlement, saying there's only the handful of pages inside and that there must be more somewhere and for me to check the ground again. So now even though I feel like taking my small implement and thrashing up the professor after all my perspiring labor, I poke my nose around and announce that's it and such is what I recall from years ago when the writing was planted.

—This is hardly even a short story, says the professor with a disappointed face. It doesn't even look finished. Twelve pages! Who would want to buy this? These are more like notes. *The Traders*, it says. Are you sure that's all there is?

I do the empty search for the third time and the professor's frown gets worse. Then like he's putting on the different clothes to fit the new occasion, Prof. M. Mittman changes up his expression.

—But at least we found something, he says, and that's what's important. Even an unpublished short story by McLemore is a significant find. And at least this won't be hard to summarize. Here take it, I don't want to see too much of it.

The professor hands me the pages but then stops like he just recalled the important detail.

—Perhaps we should film me discovering the work, he then says decisively. That might make more sense when I write about it. After all, I'm going to be describing this in great detail. Here, put this back in the ground and cover it up again, not too deep.

So now we switch the roles and Prof. M. Mittman gets down in the dirt and starts picking away with the shovel and I main control the TV camera and microphone stick. As we are doing so, a boy monk with heavy glasses comes up to eye what we are doing. He doesn't say anything, only stands beside eating the rambutans that are sticky with juice all over his robe while Prof. M. Mittman goes crawling around the ground and I press on the camera.

—Argh! I've found it! the professor then exclaims at his lungtops when he digs out the Milo jar. After all these years! The lost writings! I can't believe it!

He then stands and holds the pages up to the sun with the amazed face like he's made the shining discovery of all earth and he's the headman explorer that's been questing his whole life in the dangerous jungle. Truth be told though, it mainly looks like Prof. M. Mittman is the most terrible actor in the history of all movies in the most disbelievable picture ever, and even the boy monk is giggling to himself. Such would be damn embarrassment if any of this gets shown, I think and so I stop taking the pictures and go over to the boy monk and ask if he could now make the film of me and the professor having the discovery.

Prof. M. Mittman has the cool reaction when I suggest this but he nods all right and so the boy puts away his sticky fruits and holds up the camera and starts waving around the microphone stick. I then take the Milo pages and put such back in the ground and throw more dirt over again and I tell the boy monk to give us the ready-set-go signal.

—The boy says he'll talk now because it's the important occasion, I tell the professor. But after that, he'll take the being quiet vow again.

—Okay? I then ask the boy monk who yells out *One, two, three!* very loud and presses the camera button and this time Prof. M. Mittman and I dig up the jar at the same time, though I notice as we're doing so that the professor is aligning himself right in the middle of the boy's aim and trying to push me off to the side. But then I give another signal to the boy who screams out *One, two, three!* again and switches off the camera and now the scene is over and we all agree that this was the best believable job that we don't need to repeat.

So now we are wondering if there is any more decisive business to conduct when the boy monk speaks up.

—I want to find the jar, too! he says, declaring that it's his turn since all he got to do so far was watch. And then he puts on his eager look to the professor and me and goes over to stand by the hole. However when I tell him we cannot do since we're finished making the important report, he throws the camera and microphone stick on the ground.

—I'm missing *Let's Make the Deal!* he says before calling us the so bad ones and running off in his robes. When he gets far away, he turns around and flings a stone back at us and shouts some more before vanishing off.

After watching the boy's bursting out, the professor is quiet for a time.

—Hard to believe I've found McLemore's last work, he says at last. Obviously I hoped for more but still I feel like I'm holding literary history, like a letter by Tolstoy or a photo of Shakespeare.

And so well-preserved! It's almost like McLemore just now finished off these pages.

—He always did keep his writings up-to-date, I say.

—Yes he did, says the professor with the grave note. His work was timeless. As contemporary now as it was a hundred years ago.

The professor slowly counts the pages again.

—Still though, for such a creative mind it's odd that he left so little behind. McLemore was always a productive writer. It's not like him to turn out so little between books. His writing always came easily to him. It's almost as if he could just find the words to express what he wanted. A remarkable talent.

Prof. M. Mittman gives me the watchful look.

—You wouldn't be holding out on me now, would you? he asks. There isn't the pile of unfinished manuscripts in an old drawer somewhere, left behind to the son of an old friend? Maybe with the promise that they wouldn't be published? McLemore was such a perfectionist with his work, I can understand that happening.

I quickly shake my head.

—No, nothing like that, I say. There's nothing new he created.

—Too bad, says the professor. Just thought I'd ask.

And then Prof. M. Mittman gives the peculiar smile and we go collect the Milo jar and the camera and microphone stick and fill up all the ground holes and trudge back to the moto-bike. Before we get back on I relash the brick sack so we don't tip over and the professor opens the TV camera and takes the long picture of the surroundings.

—You know, even with all the rumors about him I never believed that McLemore was a foreign agent, he says. But being here and seeing where he lived during his last days, I now definitely get the sense he was. In fact, I'm utterly convinced beyond any doubt that McLemore was a high-level intelligence figure.

There's just something in the air here, like the grounds themselves are filled with secrets. More so than I can write about in my book. Maybe in the future someone will get to the bottom of it. What a life he must have led.

Like I do with Angry Lim, I now glimpse at the dirt to cover my improper expression. It's a long time I look there, too.

—I'm not so sure about Mr. McLemore and the intelligence business, I say at last and then we climb on the rumbly moto-bike and gasp off.

. .. .*

So now we take our never-ending home trip but at least this time the professor doesn't jump off the seat so much and when I alight him at the Heaven View House there is still some daytime left. I then see Big Yoshi, who makes the apology again to Prof. M. Mittman before the professor hurries away, and who then comes over to chin wag me about the double sword that is the tourist operation. Even though all his lodgments are full from the travelers he says, his A-1 charnel work has stopped in the tracks.

—No Tandomon persons want to die right now, says Big Yoshi in the gloomy voice, giving the look to an old *Ah Pek* inching across the street before going back inside to play with his beetles.

But now I am finally alone and so can go home to my small rooms, even if like the last time I am so drowsy that I can just reach upstairs to my bedspace. And fortunate for me Angry Lim has closed up across the street so he cannot chew my ears over the latest wearisome matters and I also see that no troubling bills have been sent today to Gecko 88 to bedraggle me. So even though I am not the drinking man, at home I take out my bottle of Chinese liquor and have a long swallow. It is the time to have the small celebration for my behalf, I think, now that my dealings with Prof. M. Mittman have the successful conclusion, every-body is winning, and there is no business left to be transacted. Although I lash myself some over why I was involved in the first place, I consider that when the professor's book is printed I will likely forget this agitation and finally see my name in print as the notable contributor. Such will be the first time I can appear in any book anywhere, *lah*, and now it is almost the certain fact, not just my wishing. And so even if Prof. M. Mittman can only create the small peanuts work, I will keep the copy up in Gecko 88 so when the purposeful customer goes to browse it I can point out where I am inside, and then maybe the person will say something of admiration and buy. And then maybe this person, too, will ask me to sign it with the gracious note and fond wishes and I will agree with the good nature, although if this situation starts to arise itself too frequently, I may have to practice my penscripting skills to create the favorable impression that will make the other persons also want to come in and buy.

However, this is as far as my considerings go since not being the drinking man I find that my big swallow has sagged me so much that I cannot even get up to throw off my dusty clothes. Maybe I should close and put away the bottle, I think, but all I can do is lay aside the paper cup and just make it across the room before I black out over across my soft bedframe.

*. *. *

And then I wake up in the early hour even though it is the long time to open Gecko 88. My muscles are still rundown and my eyes want to stay closed but for some reason I cannot help my mind from poking me with the parade of unexplainable thoughts, and so after losing this jabbing battle I raise up, change off my old clothes and pour the *kopi-o* for my breakfast.

Even so, I cannot sit down or keep from bumping about my small rooms. It is like I am anxious over the unnamed thing that is chasing me around like the invisible dog that will pounce me the moment I stop. It is a strange feeling, all right. So finally when I look outside, I see that the daylight is arriving, and I say what hell, and lock up to go early to my bookstall. Maybe then the dog can no longer hunt me around.

It is ages since I walk to my stall at this hour and now the Porridger Road is fully empty with the pink and gold lights coming up and the fresh air not yet gone stale from the cars and peoples coming later. Once the while I see the cat stalking through the alley or the old person scurrying about since they rise up early too, but elsewhere it is the quiet time that I forgot I knew about. In fact, everything looks so different that I wonder if I am familiar with this place at all, and as I go on I think about all the knowledge that even the ordinary things keep hidden from us.

However it is when I am nearly at Gecko 88 that my peaceful feeling flies off and I get the big shock. For as I am approaching closer I see that my front door is swinging open and that the yellow lamp is beaming through the window. In twenty years in the book business next July, no one has ever raided my shop, not even during the times I was selling my bushels of books for crams. Even Angry Lim was stolen the two times, but never me. And so because I am so jolted, maybe I don't stop to think about the threatening person that could be inside and just barrage in as fast as I can.

And in fact it is the nightmare scene that confronts me. First thing I see is Prof. M. Mittman sitting at the desk deeply reading a beat-up volume and twirling his spring roll fingers in his sweaty beard. His mouth is partway open as if he's in the lost trance and the air smells much *chao* like he is suffering the stomach pains and needs more of the yellow pills. But the second thing that's even worse is that Mr. McLemore's trunkcase of last things is lying open with all his writings and old books spilled out in front of the professor. And so my heart begins leaping in my mouth because I now know that Prof. M. Mittman has learned about Mr. McLemore copying his writings and that Mr. McLemore is nothing like the notable writer he wants for his project and that everything soon will be called the quits.

It's a war of feeling I'm now experiencing over whether to be ireful at Prof. M. Mittman for doing the trespass or shamed that I *sabo* him over Mr. McLemore. Either way, I consider, the truth of the situation is out of the cat bag and such is the time to suffer the deed. So the dog finally did his pounce, I think. But before I can make up my mind over which way to feel, the professor sees me standing there and puts down the dusty volume. He has the actual tears running over his face and his beak nose is twitching back and forth like the house cricket and his face is red as the sweet bean.

—It's brilliance, he says. Literature of the highest order.

At this, I cannot know what to say. Truth is, Prof. M. Mittman looks all *siao* to me, like the crack-up man the police put away and the type it is best not to engage with when they address you while walking on the street. So instead I just look at him until I cannot finally endure it any longer and have to reach around to plug in the fan to get the *chao* air flowing away from me.

—I know I shouldn't but I've been reading McLemore's work, the professor goes on. I can't help it. I've never encountered anything like it. He was a genius beyond his time. Beyond modernism, beyond postmodernism, beyond post-postmodernism. He was an anti anti-postmodernist before anti anti-postmodernism even existed.

—How did you get in?

—Broke the lock. Even I vastly underrated him. He was a visionary, a vanguard onto himself. His dynamic wholes and metonymic destability eclipse everything in modern Western literature. I've never encountered such repositional hybridity from any author.

—You mean like he stole all his writings, I say.

—His appropriation of form in the service of schematic collagism is utterly precise, utterly masterly, the professor replies. *Nestor Is My Podiatrist* is transcendent in its duplicative form. It's almost too much to speak of.

I go examine the door.

—This costs five dollars, I say.

—I'll have to owe you. The man was a revolutionary, on a par with the leading writers and thinkers in Western letters. His grasp of the purgatory of anti anti post-postmodernist cultural praxis is unparalleled. It's no wonder he died forgotten. His kind of genius can never be appreciated.

I say I deeply agree with that statement.

—I am completely humbled, says Prof. M. Mittman. Completely overawed. I never expected this kind of artistry. I can only hope... I can only hope now that I do justice to his vision.

And then the professor puts his hand over his breadloaf face like he's confronting the terrible fact he doesn't want to look up to.

—There's so much that needs to be said, so much to encompass, he says, with crying in his voice. Even his most trivial concerns are worth treatises. I don't know if I'm up to it. McLemore has given me a tremendous burden.

And now Prof. M. Mittman goes into his full plate breakdown and starts to sob away, his big head bobbing and his full self shaking like he's trapped inside the bad dream. Truth is, he reminds me of Charlie O. when Charlie O. is sometimes being like the little boy, even if Charlie O. got the real reason to cry, not like the professor who only is tremoring because he thinks he's going to do the serious work of being the notable writer not just the scholar wordplay. It must be like that for all the university persons that got to rely on the others to have their busy work to do, I think. And so I let him go on awhile before I start speaking the soothing words to calm him down, telling him not to worry since I think he's the most skilled scholar with all the powerful words and profound outlooks to make the pupils listen, and that to me, overall he and Mr. McLemore seem pretty good matched-up. That makes the professor pry his fingers off his wet face.

—Do you really think so? he asks still crying. Do you think I can give him the treatment he deserves? Am I really his equal?

I say I am fully sure of it.

—Thank you, says Prof. M. Mittman, who starts wiping away his tears with his *popiah* fingers and rinsing off his soggy beard and who is now making the air go *chao* again. That means a great deal to me, especially coming from someone who knew McLemore as long and well as you did. I'll keep your words in mind as I forge ahead, both as inspiration and admonition. My only hope now is that I haven't already read too much of his work and completely ruined my understanding of it.

XV.

How you do, I am Cecil Po for one more time. I am 63 years next August.

For the last five years I have been the very busy man, although maybe some of you know this already since to you I could be the well-known figure. Then again perhaps you are not like those people who effort to stay on top of the latest printings and book digests and notable writers, and if that is the case then I am nothing to you.

However if the person does say he knows me, it is likely because I have the connection with Mr. Lawrence L. McLemore, who became the famous Tandomon figure when the book *The Unreal Genius of Lawrence McLemore: Writer For The Ages* was printed the few years ago. Because Tandomon at that time did not possess any notable writers, such was the big event and many local persons were happy to snap up a volume like this and go around boasting of having the esteemed connection. So from this small book Mr. McLemore now is celebrated for the Tandomon people, with copies of his writings at all the mama stores and *bak kwa* shops, and his white Mr. de Gaulle face appearing on the three-cent letter stamp, and it is a prideful thing for the persons to say they have his editions, even if they never crack such open and only leave them on the high shelf to admire at.

However, because my name was also in this book as the long-time friend of Mr. McLemore that gave the many vital insights and stories about him, some of his famous attention swallowed me up, also. And so I too, began receiving the requests to talk at this or that crucial discussion or brooding symposium to give my firm opinions on Mr. McLemore's writings and the exciting accounts about being the friend. Truth is, I always enjoyed such gatherings for they reminded of Mr. Yeoh's grammars class where he put the students under his spell by reciting the arresting stories, except now I am like Mr. Yeoh. And in fact, several times I recognized in the attendance some of the *gers* I had the school with then, and who later come up to chin wag me and say nice to see you and get together soon and hand off their numbers and smile at me and what have you and so on. Even though this is not so attracting to me now.

But mostly at these significant gatherings I am talking to the curious books scholars firing me their burning questions, wanting to learn the things such as how does Mr. McLemore compose his words, or what does this exceptional passage mean, or what was in his favorite drinks? Depending on my mood and how such is posed, I can either be very courteous with the eager learner or sharp with the lazy-minded questioner who only wants to hear his voice ringing out before the others. From being the regardful speaker many times over, I can tell you that such lazy-thought persons is the biggest danger to look out for when one is addressing the crowd of hungry listeners.

But then every once in a while too, these scholars forget their questions over Mr. McLemore and ask me about the USA professor that wrote the book on him, especially since that person's sweaty picture covers the whole backside of the volume and there's also the big life story of him on the last page. Mostly they want to know how we got ourselves acquainted and if the professor is planning to research any other notable Tandomon writers.

Unfortunately, I always say, I cannot deliver them such pressing knowledge. The last time I heard of Prof. M. Mittman was the few years ago when I received the long letter asking me to congratulate him on his successful book, and also on his new job scholaring at the high-regarded Eastern USA college where he's making up the literary theory he calls Small Persons Studies. According to the professor, this type of studying inspects the world literatures for plots of the people that got repressed due to their height since in reality they were actually the short persons. There are books throughout history that are jam-pack with such accounts, he says in his letter; just take the look at the famous novel of *Anna Karenina*. According to him, this story is truly about Mrs. Karenina being the unhappy dwarf woman along with the Vronsky man in the world of average people and such is why their love had to be doomed. And such is why in the end the small person Mrs. Karenina really doesn't die by flinging herself under the train; she only dived in front of the bicycle and got hurted. It's all there in the book, he says.

But like I said, that was the last word I got from Prof. M. Mittman.

But still, even though being the regardful speaker at such chats and symposiums is the enjoyable playtime for me, you might ask, how does it make the living? What pay does it give? And normally you would be corright about this but such activities are not all I confine myself to. It's true that I still possess my bookstall twenty-five years next July, but rarely am I at Gecko 88 these days and now it is the underlings who benefact the purposeful customers wanting this famous love book or that captivating mystery novel. These days I am mainly in the schoolrooms at

Tandomon National University where I main control the Lawrence L. McLemore Institute for the Study of Literature, est. 1978. For this I have been promoted a top-class secretary and a bright bright office, and while I am not the high-rank professor lecturing before the drudging pupils, all the college teachers and striving students still come by for my fascinating analyzations of Mr. McLemore's works. Sometimes when I am especially intriguing or fired up they give the big hand when I am done and say how fortunate it is that the Tandomon National University has hired itself the esteemed authority.

To this, I always bow my head and reply Thank you and say You're being very kind and Happy you appreciate and so on, though truth is when I speak such phrases I know that I am the fortunate one, too. For among these many striving researchers who come to applaud me is the lovely Miss Tina Leung who currently is plowing her PhD in McLemore Studies at Tandomon National University and with whom I have come to share many happy hours. Each session we have together, she learns more and more over her subject and finally I have discovered why Cousin Peng has always pushed his black black tea at me.

Of course, like any burdensome position my situation is not all fun games since everyday there arises the urgent mails or demanding phone calls scattered like the seeds in the dragon fruit that even my top-class secretary cannot prevent from harassing me. And so, many times I have to say No thank you or Cannot do when the persons approach the Lawrence L. McLemore Institute for the Study of Literature est. 1978 to ask for money to build the statue of Mr. McLemore or put on the museum show about his life. But still I am the patient man when hearing these requests for even if the reply is certain to be no, one never knows if there is something else the person can say yes to.

Take for the example the message that came one day from the smart executive at the John Sanderson Literary Agency, Inc. in HK inquiring to me if I would like to pen the valuable first-person account of knowing Mr. McLemore. Such would be the big popular book, this smooth-voiced man says, and there might be the movie afterward, and then he also dropped the high-priced figure to convince me further.

Now this was the surprise call from the name I had not considered for several years and for the moment I felt some of my old feeling raising up, thinking about the smart secretary there who used to do nothing but tear up my typescripts. But despite this, I held my tongue lash and coolly replied to this persuading man that such did not interest me at the moment. However I then wondered if he would like to see some of the writings I created long ago that Mr. McLemore himself gave the great support to.

And so in the nutshell that is how *Rotten Fruits* became the Tandomon bestseller, *Don't Go Home Again* is following after that, and how I am now the notable writer you might know about years after I began my efforts and did not think such can ever occur. And while it is the mixed feeling that my writings took so long to get circulated, it still is no small thing to see one's name printed on the shiny volume in the top-notch bookstall and glimpse the people buy and carry such off. Could be it is like the parent watching their child cramming in the schoolroom or monkeying in the playground, although there is no boy or girl to grow up and later do the bad acts and give the terrible anxieties like in the case of Angry Lim. So considering this I am happy to be assured of my achievement and also escape the pounding headaches in old age that come from the growing up person. And meantime, whenever I connect to the John Sanderson Literary Agency, Inc in HK, the smart secretary answers right away and hands me off to the smart executive so they can both start kowtowing over the phone to ask when my next fascinating book is coming. Soon, I say, soon, and advise them to keep everybody's shirts on.

So with this last handful of information, now you know all the urgent facts about me for the past several years and maybe you are thinking my boresome story is finally over. Ha!, this is not yet the case for even though I am no longer the simple book-stall person like then, I am still the planning man with many fire irons. Maybe more so than ever since in this unfair life I have discovered that the more the person has, the more chances that can come his way. Like the other evening when the lovely Miss Tina Leung provided me the following piece of information that greatly stirred my thoughts and which then kept me awake alongside most of the long night.

For according to the story in *The Tandomon Talker*, there is now the big storm of worry by the English royalty persons over how to properly tribute Mr. McLemore. Because he is the notable figure that changed the course of writing and also the person that made the people think better overall of the English authors, the officials want to award him, but cannot because of the rule that says that the dead persons are outlawed from the medals or titles and can only receive the kind praises. So, says the newspaper story, there is great arguments between the officials over what to do with his memory.

Now for some reason this recalled something in me and so the next morning I hurried straightway to the Tandomon National Library est. 1914 to do my purposeful research. And there in one of the dusty volumes that have always been the friend to me I found the following vital information.

For according to one notable book, the newspaper story is corright in saying the dead persons cannot be awarded. Such is the royalty rule. But this is not the case for the living foreigners that once gave the important help to those persons. In fact, says this book writer, many foreign peoples throughout history have been honorary prized as Members, Companions, or even Knights for their deeds. Overall, he says, this is the most useful way to give the favorable publicity, while also creating the situation of harmonious feeling with the colony nations. He calls it the good use of *noblesse oblige.*

Now I never before heard the name of the worthy writer making this intriguing conclusion, and although I scan more dusty volumes I don't see him listed any further. Maybe he was like me once and laying under rocks or maybe he is like Mr. McLemore and not really the book writer at all, only a careful copier. For who really knows who is the creator behind the book? But no matter, his crucial statement provoked in me right away the immediate good idea. So as the result, tomorrow morning before I begin my significant duties at the Lawrence L. McLemore Institute for the Study of Literature est. 1978, I will be pulling out my A-1 stationery and best biro and composing my careful letter to the Queen to inform her fully about how she can resolve this highly urgent matter. After all my efforts I am thinking, Sir Cecil Po is the best name for this very notable writer.

Acknowledgments

For this book, many thanks to editor Diane, life friend CG, and daughter Pilar.

Photo: Claire Calderon

Scott Shibuya Brown is the author of the novel *Far Afield* (Red Hen Press, 2010), and a former staff journalist at *Time Magazine* and *The Los Angeles Times*. His reporting, reviews, and photos also have appeared in *The Atlantic Monthly*, *The Washington Post*, *The Kartika Review* and *The LA Weekly*, among other publications. He has an MFA in Writing from CalArts and currently teaches at California State University, Northridge. He lives in Los Angeles and is currently working on a novel set in 1950s Japan.